iN THE BREAK

LITTLE, BROWN AND COMPANY

New York ⚬ Boston

IN THE BREAK

a novel by **JACK LOPEZ**

Little, Brown and Company

Time Warner Book Group
1271 Avenue of the Americas, New York, NY 10020
Visit our Web site at www.lb-teens.com

First Edition: July 2006

Epigraph quote from *Island of the Blue Dolphins* by Scott O'Dell,
1960, Houghton Mifflin Company.

Library of Congress Cataloging-in-Publication Data
López, Jack.
   In the break / by Jack López. — 1st ed.
      p.   cm.
   Summary: Surfing is Juan Barrela's life but when his best friend Jamie
faces a violent home situation, the tenth-grader steals his mother's car and
drives with Jamie's sister Amber to Mexico to help her brother hide until
tragedy strikes the trio.
   ISBN 0-316-00874-5 (hardcover : alk. paper)
   [1. Surfing — Fiction. 2. Best friends — Fiction. 3. Friendship — Fiction.
4. Mexican Americans — Fiction. 5. Family life — California — Fiction.
6. California — Fiction.]   I. Title.
PZ7.L876355In 2006
[Fic] — dc22

                                                        2005015082

                           10 9 8 7 6 5 4 3 2 1

                                  Q-FF

                  Printed in the United States of America

  The text was set in Manticore, and the display type is BulletinGrunge.

For my mother, *Agripina Estavillo Lopez*

A WAVE PASSED OVER MY HEAD AND I WENT DOWN AND DOWN UNTIL

I thought I would never behold the day again.

—Scott O'Dell, *Island of the Blue Dolphins*

CHAPTER 1

"Juan."

No answer.

"Juan."

No answer.

"What's with you, Juan?"

I wanted to sleep!

"Psssst! C'mon, swell's up." Half whisper, not his normal voice.

"Shut up."

Normal voice: "Get up, asshole."

"Okay, okay. Keep it down." It was Sunday morning, and my mother and father liked to sleep late. Everybody was supposed to keep quiet, not supposed to have friends come to their windows and shout out for the whole damn house to hear.

"I'll get your board."

"Yeah." I put the pillow over my head and went back to sleep. Then Jamie began honking the horn! I looked at the clock. It wasn't even 6:30. I looked at my older brother's twin bed, empty, unused.

On the way out of the house I saw my little brother already catatonic in front of the TV — anime or something. No, it was too early for those shows, and, besides, they were on Saturdays. "Paul, tell 'em I went surfing."

He grunted without looking at me. Twerp seven-year-olds!

I threw my pack in the backseat on top of our boards that Jamie had stuffed in . . . F's car? "What are you doing with F's ride?"

"My mom's car's dead."

I didn't like this one bit. "Does F know?"

"Screw F," Jamie said, putting the car in gear and peeling out.

I had to chuckle. F, Jamie's so-called stepdad, (Frederick was his name, but our nickname for him was Fuckhead and F was what we called him) was such an ass, he deserved to have his car taken. But the funniest thing was, had Jamie shown up in his mother's car, which he usually did, I wouldn't have thought a thing of it, even though he only had a learner's permit. He always drove as if he had a license and his own car. But now, it really did seem illegal, somehow, what we were doing.

I looked over at Jamie. He had the seat way back so he'd be low in it, though his legs were still scrunched at the knees. His hair was all messed up and blowing in the wind. Even though there was a chill in the early morning air, he had the windows down.

"What?" he said, and then laughed his high-pitched laugh. It was like a weird hiccup or something.

I shook my head.

"You won't do that when you see the waves."

"There aren't any waves."

"Greg J.'s getting it right now."

"No, he's not. Did they go?"

"You bet they did."

Greg J.'s father surfed and took Greg J. and his older brother down to Baja. Greg J. was on the surf team, he had a huge expensive house, and his dad had customized a van for Baja surf trips. I think his grandfather even surfed, dammit! He wasn't our friend.

A hurricane swell was on the way. But it was too soon for the waves to be here, or so the buoy readings said last night when I checked them online. "They're not getting anything this weekend."

"You gotta believe, Juan."

"I do. In surfcams."

We dropped down the hill, turned left on the Coast Highway, passing sandy Playa Chica, heading toward the pier. On the mesa where we lived you could smell the ocean air, but when you got closer it permeated everything. There would be one more even stronger blast right before you got in the water. It was funny, I knew where Jamie was headed even though we hadn't talked about it. There was a sandbar right in front of Greg Scott's street. It had built all summer, and now, with the approaching big swell from the south, it would fire!

When we could see the waves, Jamie said, "Fuck."

I knew it. "Swell's going to hit tomorrow. Maybe, if we're really lucky, a little action this afternoon." You can get all the info you need online.

"Tomorrow's school." He parked the car; we got our boards and stuff, and walked down the sand to the water's edge. The surf was little.

On the paddle out we could see who was in the water (Greg Scott, Ricky Ybarra, Herbie French, a bunch of other guys I didn't really know, and some old longboarders), what the tide and the waves were doing (dropping tide, dinky waves), and how the crowd was (big for so early, soon to get bigger). One good thing about surfing is that the waves almost always seem smaller from shore than when you enter the water. Sure, these waves were small, but they were hollow from the dropping tide, and would only get faster.

"Yeah!" Jamie shouted to Greg Scott as he crouched and got covered and then scrunched in the shorebreak. He broke the surface and looked at Jamie and me. "It's about time," he said, jumping on his board. As Greg Scott paddled, Jamie caught up to him, tugged on his leash and kept pulling, and passed him by pushing off his body. Greg Scott hadn't been expecting this, and I too caught up to him and propelled myself by grabbing on to him and thrusting myself forward, paddling hard to catch Jamie.

"Pricks!" he shouted as he got hit by an incoming wave.

We paddled out to the sandbar ahead of Greg Scott, scoping out the lineup. Boom — in no time some little lines showed, and Jamie caught the first one, acing out some older guy who'd been there first but didn't have position on Jamie. The guy whistled his disapproval. Jamie looked back just before dropping in, staring at the guy.

That was the problem with surfing around older guys: they thought that just because they were older, you were supposed to cut them some slack. On the next wave I out-positioned the dude, and he really whistled. After my ride and on my way back out I saw the same guy go ballistic when Herbie shoulder-hopped him. Who gave a shit, we were surfing!

CHAPTER 2

Paddling back out yet again, I watched Jamie take off, stalling his board at the top. When he shot down the line and some guy dropped in on him I tensed, though the kook flopped off his board. Jamie was still in a good mood. Had the kook pissed him off and been older, Jamie might have thrown down with him in the shallow water. By the time the whitewater from that wave got to me, I pushed through the measly remnants.

It had remained a clear, calm morning, unusually warm even for late September, and particularly crowded, though it was what you'd expect for a Sunday. I was tired but took off anyway on the next wave: waist-high mush. I faded left, cranked a turn when I hit the bottom, going right. There was no juice to it, so I turned back into the whitewater, bellying the pathetic thing all the way into shore. I picked up my board and walked through the swirling water up the incline onto the white sand, where Amber, Jamie's sister, sat with Robert Bonham. The sea was now riffled with the rising wind, and

Jamie was paddling back out to the lineup, toward our friends. I placed my board on Amber's.

Turning back and facing the sea, I scanned north toward the bluffs and then all the way south to the pier. There wasn't much of a swell. The tide was coming up as was the crowd, making the surfing day over. Whitewater hit the pier's pilings with a gentle regularity, and tourists dotted the top of the structure. I stretched my arms over my head and swiveled side to side. Then I grabbed my towel and looked at Amber and Robert. Bad vibe. Fighting vibe, which they'd been doing a lot of recently. Amber sat on her beach towel, looking out to the break, fidgeting with her Hello Kitty backpack, which she always had with her, it seemed. In it she kept her journal, and shells and beach glass and all kinds of shit that she was always collecting on the beach, feathers and rings and all sorts of trinkets. Robert stood beside her, looking toward the pier.

Amber was so pigeon-toed that her feet actually crossed over in front of each other as she walked. But they never collided, though it appeared that they should. Even when she surfed. She never wore shoes in the daytime, only at night. When it was warm as it was now she surfed in board shorts and a bikini top with a rash guard, which she now wore, sitting on her towel. She always had a deep copper tan, the result of much thought and patience, of lying on the beach or in the sun for hours, moving her towel so it would face the right direction, rotating her body so that it tanned evenly, and even going so far as to lie on her sides an equal amount of time as she lay on her back and stomach. She didn't speak a lot until she knew you, and even then she was not particularly talkative. She was tall, long-legged, and strong. She never wore any makeup, and a lot of girls didn't, but in her case guys thought she was weird; I think they were afraid of her. She was imposing, regal in her quiet beauty. She had gotten straight A's so far through high school, and was planning on going to Berkeley or Stanford when she graduated. The only boyfriend she ever had was Robert Bonham, the dirty dog (how I envied him!). From the ninth grade on she was his girlfriend. He was attending community college. Amber was in the twelfth grade, two grades ahead of Jamie and me.

Now, as she sat on the beach above the high-tide line, looking uncomfortable and sad, her feet, even while sitting, were pigeon-toed.

"The hell with this," Robert Bonham said, and stomped off toward the service road at the end of the beach.

"Nice," I said. Supposedly Robert Bonham had been with another girl, or that's the story I heard. He and Amber had been going at it for a few weeks now.

Amber stuck her tongue out and crossed her eyes at me.

Don't, I thought, it'll make your eyes crossed permanently, like your feet.

The wind was picking up for real now, and I wrapped the towel around my upper body. Amber'd missed the good waves of the morning, sitting on the beach and arguing with Robert Bonham. I'd rather surf than argue with a girlfriend.

Jamie continued surfing, even though it was getting really windy. He caught wave after wave, no matter how bumpy the faces were, trying to perform some tricks: floaters, big cutbacks, getting tiny air when he could, all the things you do when you surf crummy waves but you yourself are really good.

"Oh crap!" Amber said.

I didn't turn around, assuming that Robert Bonham was back.

"Where is he?" a stern and angry voice half-shouted.

There stood F in a white shirt and tie, slacks, and hard shoes, right on the sand! In all his imposing size and heft. It wasn't that F was really that big, or that he was obese or anything. He just looked big, what with his fat head and his meaty forearms. He gave the appearance of being larger than he actually was. I looked out to sea, ignoring him.

"I know he's here, and he took my car," F said. "He was supposed to mow the lawn!"

"I drove," Amber said. She had come with Robert, about an hour after Jamie and I had.

"Don't you lie to me. Don't!" Other sunbathers and surfers began looking at us.

Amber said nothing. She wrapped her arms around her shoulders, trying unsuccessfully to make herself smaller somehow.

"He didn't ask permission to use my car! He was supposed to mow the lawn on *Friday!* Get him in. Now!"

I looked at F in all his crew-cut, engineer fury. He was a full dick, but he was scary. Especially when he was pissed off, which was practically all the time. I only saw him around Jamie, and he seemed perpetually pissed at him. Jamie could do no right as far as F was concerned. So he would yell at Jamie about the car, and, when you got down to it, he'd been yelling since shortly after he married Claire, Amber and Jamie's mother. I suppose F had been auditioning for the family before he married into it when he pretended to be nice to Jamie, pretended he gave a shit about surfing, or any of the stuff that other fathers are interested in. I didn't have to take his orders, but didn't want any undue grief to befall Amber, so I walked out toward the surf and began waving to Jamie.

As I tried to get his attention I wondered why it was we got stuck with the people we got stuck with? Me, I was lucky, I guess. My parents irritated the hell out of me sometimes. But they cared about me. They wanted me to do the right thing and they did right by me. F not only didn't care about Jamie, he wanted to break him or something, like a drill instructor in those goofy movies. The guys in the movies can't do anything about it cause they're in the Army, and I guess Jamie's in the same boat because he can do nothing either, until he moves out — which will be the second he's eighteen, maybe before, I know that much. When I finally caught his eye he flipped me off, though I kept waving to him. After about ten minutes he rode a wave in.

Jamie smiled his winning smile at me, throwing his long, sandy-blond hair back out of his eyes. He was tall and thin, though when he got older he was going to be huge. The football coaches were always trying to get him to join the team. "Why you buggin' me, Juan?" he said, laughing. His voice was a little higher when he laughed.

"F's here."

"Ah, crap."

"He's giving Amber shit."

All the joy disappeared from Jamie's face and he looked empty yet determined as he went up the beach, dropping his board in the sand next to mine.

Before I knew what happened, he stood before F, arms crossed over his chest, head down, supplicatory, as if he were in the principal's office or something.

11

"Who gave you permission to take *my* car?"

Jamie didn't say anything, just stood there, looking at the sand.

"Who, goddamit!"

"No one," Jamie said, now looking right in F's face.

"What about the lawn? Why don't you do anything? And your lousy grades. Let me tell you something, after your prank this morning, your free ride's over!"

Jamie just stood there taking it, that asshole yelling right in his face before the whole world to see. I don't know why I was set in stone but I was. Amber wasn't though. She jumped up, getting in between them, saying, "Not here, Frederick."

When F made like he was going to grab her, Jamie gave him a ferocious shove, knocking him on his ass. But F was quick in spite of his age and size, and he grabbed Jamie while going down. They tussled, rolling in the sand like dogs, F punching Jamie on the head, the back, the shoulders. When they stood up, Jamie held his hand over his nose and I could see blood leaking out. In an instant F had Jamie by his free wrist, dragging him up the beach toward the cars.

"Ahhhhhhhh!" Amber shrieked. While sitting on the sand she said, almost to herself, "I hate you." She pulled her knees up to her chest and buried her face between her knees.

It was brutal and quick, and everybody in close proximity looked at us. Jamie and F were now climbing the small bluff right before Coast Highway. In an instant they were gone. Where was that ass Robert Bonham when we needed him? He could stand up to F, was legally an adult. When I looked down at Amber, she was crying, her hands covering her face.

I felt sick but also felt like doing something, so I picked up Jamie's board and walked it back down into the surf, rinsing it off. While thinking of Jamie I sat back on the sand, away from Amber, and watched the surf deteriorate.

I had been in only one fight in my life. And it was because of Jamie. When we were in the third grade there was a wacko named Alex who always picked on kids and stuff. At that time Jamie was so shy that he couldn't even do his book reports in front of the class; he would stay after school and do them in front of the teacher. I could watch if I wanted, and I usually did. At that time he wouldn't stand up for himself at all. It was only later that he would assert himself for what was right.

This one day we were lined up on the ramp waiting for Mrs. Brown, our third-grade teacher, to arrive when Alex cut in front of Jamie. Jamie let him. No problem. But then Alex turned around and started flicking Jamie on the head.

"Stop it," Jamie said after a few more flicks had hit him.

That was ammunition for Alex to flick him harder.

School had just begun and September was always the hottest month, though there were olive trees shielding us from the morning sun. And Mrs. Brown had to be late this day of all days.

Alex flicked Jamie again, really hard.

Jamie just looked down at that ground.

"Cut it out," I said to Alex. Other kids were now watching.

Alex flicked Jamie again.

What enraged me was to see Jamie flinch before he was even hit. I pushed Alex hard on his shoulder.

He came forward, trying to flick my head, but I just kicked him in the stomach, the way I'd seen these Thai kickboxers do on television. Nestor, my father, would sometimes watch sports on TV before he went to work and I'd watch with him. The kickboxers just wailed on each other using their hands, feet, knees, and elbows even. I noticed when they came forward they led with a kick, a lifting of the knee and snap of the foot. That was what I did to Alex. And it caught him right in the belly.

Right when Mrs. Brown showed up.

Jamie was as surprised as I was that Alex was suddenly crying. I was sent to the principal's office, where my only regret was that I cried too when she told me how much trouble I was in.

Now, I almost felt like crying. Rather than help Jamie moments ago, I had just stood by. Amber was the one who had intervened, not I.

After some time she said, "That's why he wasn't at school." She stared at the waves and her voice sounded scratchy.

Jamie had told me he didn't feel well, was why he missed school on Friday. "What?"

"F wouldn't let him out of the house until he mowed the lawn. He wouldn't do it Friday and he wouldn't do it yesterday. He just sat in his room. Until this morning."

We had talked on the phone and he'd said he didn't feel like doing anything. But the hurricane swell got him off his ass. And it wasn't even here yet. I didn't know what to say so I said nothing.

Some of our friends came in from the water, though most of them hadn't seen anything. Greg Scott had but he was too polite to mention it. I could tell by the way he looked at Amber that he knew. In fact, everyone knew that F was an asshole and yelled at Jamie sometimes. Nobody talked about it, it was just growing-up shit. F was a cheap jerk. Jamie was big now. Some shit would go down, no doubt about it.

While picking up my board I told Amber we should go. She got her board, stuffed her towel into her backpack, and, in a slight daze, followed me, Greg Scott walking with us. When we got up to the highway, there was no car. F must have taken it.

"Now what?" Amber said. Her long brown hair was coming out of its tight braid. Her face looked more linear than it really was, making her look older, tired.

"You can leave your boards at my house," Greg Scott said. He was such a pal, unlike Mr. Has-It-All Greg J.

And we did, which was nothing new. I carried my board under my right arm, and Jamie's under my left arm. An hour ago we had two cars. Now we had no car and four boards to carry. Greg Scott's father saw us approaching and came out and took Jamie's board from me, helping us to place them all in the garage.

"Where's Jamie?" Mr. Scott said.

"He had to get home suddenly," Greg Scott said. He looked at his father. His father asked no more questions.

I didn't feel like carrying my pack all the way back home, so I left it with the boards. Amber left her wetsuit and stuff too.

Greg Scott walked with us back to the street. His father resumed the weeding he was doing. "Take it easy," Greg Scott said.

"Yeah," I said. Then Amber and I began the long walk back toward our houses.

CHAPTER 3

Behind The Strand, the name of the beach houses just north of Playa Chica, were large tract homes where Jamie lived. His father, Mr. Watkins, had been a really nice guy, coming to our ball games when we were young, putting a basketball backboard in their driveway and shooting hoops with us far into those summer nights that seemed to go on forever when I used to spend the night at Jamie's. His house was bike-riding distance from mine, and he and I spent all our free time together.

For a time I think I secretly wanted to be a Watkins, to be their second son, to have those soft searing blue eyes that Jamie and Amber had, to have the sandy blond hair, to be in a two-child family, to acquire the ease with which they all seemed to do everything. Jamie's father was a professional, an up-and-coming architect, someone who was in the paper sometimes for awards and things. Mrs. Watkins was athletic and perky (my mother's term — I think she was jealous), and stayed home.

My parents were the same age as Jamie's, but they were not Claire and Eddie. My father was a printer, my mother a secretary, and sometimes they fought over not having enough money. There were four kids in my family and money was tight. Our land was worth a lot, though, and that was something.

I was thinking all this shit as I tried to get comfortable on the shower floor, where I always fell asleep. I don't know why, but I liked to nap with the water cascading over me. I liked the tingling feeling the jets of spray made as they hit my head; I liked the warm, safe feeling I had inside the shower, locked inside the bathroom. None of my family could disturb me here. While leaning my legs up against the opposite tile wall I couldn't help thinking about this morning at the beach.

"Hurry up, I need to pee!" my little sister shouted from the other side of the door.

"Go away!"

"I'm telling, you're not supposed to stay in the shower so long," Patti whined.

"Okay, I'll be out in a minute," I lied. I listened to see if she was actually going to tell, which she rarely did. She could use the other bathroom, dammit! In time, I forgot about her threat, the warm water making me drowsy.

Jamie and I had met in kindergarten. One day Mrs. Watkins approached my mother, asking if it was okay for me to come and play at their house. Of course it was, but, still, my mother had to go over and check things out just for form's sake. From that time on we had a regular play day — Tuesday — which lasted through elementary school.

After Mr. Watkins died, Tuesdays turned into every day, because I would walk home with Jamie and hang with him. Mr. Watkins died in a freeway auto accident. He was driving early in the morning on his way to a shopping-center site that his firm was going to design. A big rig crashed over the center divider and hit Mr. Watkins's car head on. He died on impact, the Highway Patrol told Mrs. Watkins. He hadn't suffered, they said. And his car had hit others, three more people dying in the fiery crash. The Highway Patrol said the stuff about dying instantly because there was a horrific fire, and not much was left of some of the accident victims. It was all right there on the freeway, and on television and in the newspapers, really sucking in its gory details.

Jamie was in the fifth grade, Amber in seventh. People from all over the area attended the funeral, and so did I and my parents. Even my older brother went because he knew the family, and my father said he should pay his respects.

At that time it was no longer fun to go over to Jamie's, but I still did. He started coming over to my house more often, and I knew it was hard for him to see my father, but that was what he wanted, to hang around somebody else's father, I guessed.

My legs were above my head, my back flat on the floor, which stopped the drain, I noticed, as water was almost overflowing the shower pan, so I switched positions, leaning against the wall and pulling up my knees into my chest so the water hit my neck and back as I stretched my upper body forward. I settled in, thinking how hard it had been for Jamie to lose his father, to lose all his money, to have F live in his house.

Sick shit, I figured, because of a damn big rig.

I must have finally conked out, thinking those thoughts, letting the hot water soak me, when my father, Nestor Barrela, banged on the bathroom door. My older brother Raul, when he first began to talk, had called him Nestor Barrela, and it had sort of stuck as a family joke, though I just called him by his first name. "You're using all the hot water!" Nestor shouted. When he wasn't home I wouldn't wake up until the cold water hit me.

After drying off, I lay on my bed in my room. My brother's bed was still against the other wall, and I could almost imagine him lying there in his boxers, talking on his cell, his lean and strong body gangly-like even though he wasn't that tall, his brown hair still messed up from showering, his long eyelashes looking wet though they weren't. I'd shared a room with him my entire life, and now he was married and going to be a father. It was weird not having his clothes in the closet, not having stuff I could borrow if I needed it. Or not talking with him when he came home from his job at the pharmacy, where he had worked the counter and made deliveries.

I must have dozed off again, for the next thing I knew my mother said, "Come on, sleepy head." She was *in* my room.

"I'll be right there."

It was weird with only five of us at the table, my older brother's seat empty next to me. Across from me sat my little sister and brother. Patti was eleven, Paul seven, still getting his "big" teeth. My older brother was nineteen (soon to be twenty), four and a half years older than me.

"How was surfing?" Nestor said. Even though my mother wasn't yet seated, he'd already begun eating.

My mother had made meatloaf and mashed potatoes and gravy. But my parents put salsa on their meatloaf, something none of my friends' parents did. And my father would sometimes wrap the meat in a tortilla, making a small burrito. Another thing my friends didn't do. Ever. But they tasted good that way and I did the same as my father.

"How was it?" my father asked again.

I thought of Jamie. "It was fun for a while," I said.

"You sure were tired," my mother said, placing the gravy bowl on the table and sitting down. "It's not like you to sleep all afternoon. Are you feeling well?" She placed her hand on my forehead.

I recoiled from her touch. I didn't tell them about walking home, about F and Jamie on the beach.

"He's fine, just lazy." Nestor was half finished with his food before we'd even served ourselves.

"No, I'm not," I said.

Nestor bared his teeth at me, his teasing smile.

"Leave him alone," my mother said. As she chewed she always ground her teeth, something that made me squirm, sort of like when you hear chalk screech over the blackboard.

My sister wolfed down her food, following my father's lead, laughing from time to time. She was starting to develop already, and she was going to be real pretty, like my mother. My mother was short with a "full figure" and a bright smile and she colored her hair a reddish shade. My sister had brown hair and green eyes and the fair skin of our mother.

My father, finished with his food, pushed his plate forward, stood up, and said, "I'm going to read." That meant he was going to take a nap before going to work. He was a printer, a foreman, and he worked the graveyard shift, eleven at night until seven in the morning, but he had a far drive to get to work, and he always went in early on Sunday night, the first work night of the week for workers of the graveyard shift.

As we finished our dinner, my mother said to me, "Are you okay? You're awfully quiet."

"Mom, can I get a subscription to *CosmoGirl?*" Patti said.

"I'm okay," I said.

"I want my own computer," Paul said.

"You're too young," I said.

"Nobody's getting anything," my mother said.

"I'm gonna go shoot baskets," I said. My mother gave me the stare. "May I please be excused?"

It was around sunset when I climbed on top of the block wall that surrounds our backyard and looked out to sea. From a standing position on the wall, I could see the surfline at Playa Chica. The waves did seem to be building — there was a solid line of white-water crashing on shore. Cool. Tomorrow would be good. But tomorrow was a school day. Monday. Maybe I could fake being sick.

I sat on the wall, watching the colors of the sky as they transitioned from day to night, from bright and textured to dark and flat. When it was almost dark, I went inside the house.

⚬❀⚬

A theme song for some bogus reality show was going when I thought I heard something outside. My mother was asleep. Because she worked in the morning, she'd go to bed early. Nestor had already left for work, taking his old Toyota pickup. My younger brother and sister were asleep, since they went to bed at 9:00. Probably the wind. It had been really blowing when I came in at sunset.

I sort of had the house to myself and was enjoying it. I had some homework to do, had to study for a test, print out an assignment for English, nothing to get excited over. I liked to stay up late and do my schoolwork when the house was quiet. The problem was that I aced everything without trying; I just wasn't challenged, as Mr. Vance, my homeroom teacher said. I was considering skipping eleventh grade next year and going right to twelfth, if this year stayed so boring. The problem was that Jamie wasn't in the H classes — the honors classes — and I'd be a grade ahead of him, and I'd graduate a year before him. I resisted last year when my counselor, Mrs. Perez, had approached my parents. I'll give this to Nestor and my mother, they don't force things on me that I don't want. As the theme song continued playing I went into the kitchen to get a bowl of ice cream. I thought I heard a tap at the front door, but ignored it because nobody would come over on Sunday night. I plopped back down on the sofa, spooning ice cream down my gullet, with all the big, comfortable pillows propping me up. There it was again. Tap, tap, very lightly. And again.

What the? I thought on my way to the door and opened it.

"Juan," Amber hissed. She wore a T-shirt and her frayed cutoff Levi's and her hair was all messed up and she was way out of breath and it looked as if she'd been crying. She held her hands together, wringing them, a gesture I'd never seen her do, making her backpack fall off her shoulder.

I hated to admit it, but after dinner I had forgotten about the shit this morning. Overcoming my surprise, I said, "Come in." I could count on the fingers of my right hand the times Amber had been over, and I couldn't ever remember when she was here on her own.

"No," she said. She was breathing hard, as if she'd been running, but she was trying to mask it so she'd be quiet.

I'd always had a crush on Amber. And now here she was at my door, her chest heaving up and down and her powerful and perpetually tanned legs twitching into a pigeon-toed stance. Her individual features were angular, sharp, and she shouldn't be good-looking, but she was. She was beautiful, in my opinion. It wasn't that Amber was so stunningly good-looking or an outrageous babe or anything. But once you saw her you wouldn't forget; her beauty was not ordinary.

After she caught her breath she said, "Jamie's on the beach. He beat the shit out of F."

"Come in."

"I'm taking him money. He got some stuff together and left. He asked me to get you."

"Where's F now?"

"I'm not sure. My mother called the paramedics. I think the cops'll come too."

"Crap. Get in." I leaned forward and grabbed her arm, pulling her into the entry hall. I turned off the porch light. "Let me get a sweatshirt."

Jamie was in trouble. My best friend in big trouble, the sinking feeling right in my gut told me.

Moments later we ran across the field over the hollows, underground trenches for storing World War II munitions. Sometimes kids would hang out at the hollows when they were avoiding their parents.

A slight overcast blew in off the ocean, obscuring the half moon that washed the land in an eerie light. The smell of saltwater permeated the air, and Amber and I were huffing and puffing, but still, we ran toward the sea. It was just beyond the marsh, beyond the four-lane highway that skirted the beach and went all the way to the pier, all the way to Mexico.

"Wait," Amber said. She leaned over, panting.

"You okay?" I said.

Her braid fell over her head, almost hitting the ground. She stood upright, gave me a sad smile, and pushed me. "Yeah. F was drunk, Juan. Drunk! And yelling at all of us. Jamie stood up to him and kicked his ass. He hurt him. F's hurt, I mean really hurt."

"Let's go!" We took off again.

After we'd made it through the strawberry field and through the cornfield we slowed to climb down the small sandstone cliff that would put us on the marsh. The cornstalks rustled in the night breeze, and it was as if you could hear the tidal movement through the marsh — the tide would recede for another hour. There was nothing to do but wade through the muck, which sucked at our feet as we trudged on. Soon the water was up to our knees, then our waists, and at this point you could really feel the tidal current wanting to take you out to sea.

"He's got a gun at the house. He said he'd kill Jamie." Amber huffed long, deep breaths as we stopped again.

My family was probably the only one in the nation not to have an arsenal of firepower at our disposal in our house. In fact, my family was totally old school. I couldn't have piercings, tattoos, iced hair, cell, and my brother married his girlfriend just because she was pregnant. My father told my brother that he was doing the right thing. I thought he was a chump, even though I liked Bonnie.

"If F was drinking, maybe he'll cool down," I said after thinking about it.

"F's messed up. He was, like, convulsing on the floor."

Soon we slogged through the shallow marshy part in front of the Coast Highway, and stopped before crossing. This was potentially dangerous because if cops were looking for Jamie and saw us crossing, then they could get to him.

"I don't know if we should both go at once or separately," I said to Amber.

She knew what I referred to because she said with no hesitation, "At the same time. Otherwise there'd be two chances to see us."

She was right, of course, and I wondered why I wasn't thinking so clearly. Fact of the matter was, I was scared. At first I thought I was only scared for Jamie. Then I knew my fear was for Amber as well. Now, this minute, as I prepared to cross the Coast Highway, I knew that I was also scared for myself. What if F had his gun and was coming for Jamie? I didn't want to die by gunshot, I wanted to drown in huge waves. Waves that were totally out of control. Fucking chaos!

As we caught our breath I thought about F. He didn't like me anymore. At first he seemed to, but more recently he'd try to bait me into arguing with him, and had even used a racial slur to intimidate me. I knew that if he ever went too far, I'd tell my father, and my father would stand up to the dick, kick the royal shit out of him, should it come to that. But now my father wasn't around. Besides, Jamie had already kicked his ass.

"Well," I said, "we'd better get to it."

"Let's wait for a good break," Amber said.

When it came we sprinted across the highway and then lay in the sand off the road, not far from the asphalt. A few cars whizzed by, nothing out of the ordinary. After a time of catching our breath, we sprinted the long sandy beach to the water's edge, where Jamie should be.

The overcast was in strong, small cloud wisps rushing past our faces as we stood right above the shoreline. Amber began yelling for Jamie, but he never would have heard her, what with the roar of the breaking waves and the onshore wind. Her words were just blown about like whitecaps far out at sea. As I looked at her, she was peering out onto the black ocean, and I felt a sudden urge to hold her.

But I said, "Let's split up; I'll go north, you go south."

"No," Amber said. "We're not separating." The tone in her voice made it final, and she took my arm, placing her hand in mine and pulled me forward with her.

First we walked north, calling for Jamie. When we got pretty close to The Strand and the houses on the sand, we turned back. Walking south, I began looking up on the mesa for my house. There were only a few other buildings on the huge flat piece of ground overlooking Playa Chica. Our neighbors were horse people, and I could see the lights from the various barns and houses surrounding my own house.

When we were south of the mesa we found Jamie. He was sitting in the sand shivering. Amber hugged him. She tried to give him my sweatshirt, which I'd gotten for her, but he refused, and it wouldn't have fit anyway.

"Did you see anything? Cops or . . ." His voice was hoarse and nasal as it trailed off.

"No." I wasn't lying; I hadn't seen anything, and I was on high alert for sirens.

The wind was howling, and it seemed to be blowing the tops of waves right on us: I felt damp inside and my hair was wet. We sat in silence, comfortable in each other's company, knowing there was no good solution to Jamie's problem. The high-tide surge was almost up to where we sat.

"I'm going to hitchhike south," Jamie said. "I can't stay here."

"Only psychos hitchhike," Amber said.

"I've got to get out of here. I'm not getting arrested for that prick."

Silence.

"What if the cops are driving Coast Highway?" Jamie on the highway with only the beach for cover, which was no protection at all, wasn't a scenario that I relished.

"It's cool, there's nothing else to do," Jamie said with a resigned quality to his voice that I'd not heard before. It was acceptance and calmness at the same time.

Amber pulled Jamie into her shoulder.

"What's going on, guys? I mean, shit's happening pretty fast. Jamie, you fought F?"

"Yeah, I did." He sounded as if his tongue was too thick or something, making his words raspy and soft at the same time. "I kicked his ass. I surprised him. He went off on me twice and I didn't respond. This time, I nailed him right in the throat and got him on the floor and worked out on his face. I fucked him up. I hit him and hit him and kept hitting him. And you know what? It felt really good. I mean, really."

"It was ugly, Juan. I hate F, but I don't want Jamie to . . ."

"Be killed by that fucker," Jamie filled in.

"No, get arrested. You wailed on him. It's different now, Juan. F's weird or crazy or something. He changed big time."

"He takes everything out on me," Jamie said. "And I'm through with it."

Amber removed her arm from around Jamie's shoulder and sat up straight.

She had always protected him, especially after their father died. She had a fierce protective net around Jamie, always looking out for him, once even challenging a bully who was giving Jamie and me shit after school. We were in the first grade and thought it was very cool.

One time when I was with Jamie in his room shortly after his father died, he started crying. I didn't know what to say, didn't know what to do, but Amber came in and held him. Simply held him and they both cried. I left, letting myself out of the house and walking home in a sad daze. At that time she made it a point to keep a close eye on him, to spend time with him when I wasn't around, even taking him with Robert Bonham when they went to Disneyland on one of their first dates.

When Amber started surfing she insisted that Robert take Jamie and me along sometimes, even though we'd been at it for a few years already. And he did, surfing with us down the coast at breaks we would never have been able to get to.

When F entered the scene, Amber took up the void left by Mrs. Watkins's defection. It wasn't that their mom neglected Jamie or anything. She was just spending time with a man, a guy who wasn't Jamie's father, and I knew Jamie didn't like it, though he never said anything about it. He kept quiet, as usual. But it was weird — I could know stuff about Jamie without us ever talking about it. I knew he didn't like F being with his mother. I knew he wasn't happy when she eloped with him. But what could he do?

Could he really get arrested?

We sat there quiet, gazing out over the dark sea. In the silent roar of the waves breaking by the shore I wondered how I could help. I couldn't see their faces, couldn't gauge their emotions, but it was as if Amber had read my mind.

"F hid the car keys," she said.

Jamie shouted, "The dick locked them in his safe."

I wondered why Jamie hadn't just taken his mother's car, then remembered it wasn't running, the reason he'd taken F's in the first place to get us to the morning waves. "Maybe I can get my mother's car," I said. A plan was formulating in my mind.

"Could you?" Amber said.

"Your mother won't give you her car," Jamie said.

"I won't ask."

We digested the implications of that remark. Remembering the warmth of Amber's hand in mine, I thought, I could do it. My father was at work — he wouldn't be home until eight in the morning, and my mother was a heavy sleeper. Besides, I didn't want Jamie to go through any more shit. Not tonight.

"It's just to get Jamie out of town, get him a good start." I'll get the car back before my father gets home from work and before my mother wakes up, I thought.

"I'll go with you," Amber said.

ᏒᏙ

It was after midnight as Amber drove my mother's car. I was pensive in the passenger seat — I'd never done anything close to this my entire life! We drove in the Barrela family car, a brand-new 4Runner cruising next to the beach without letting the tires go into the sand. Tourists always tried to drive up on the beach to park, and when it was time to go they'd gun their engines and spin their tires, expecting the sand to release them, but the sand was unforgiving. It was tricky driving because Amber had turned off the headlights so as not to be seen from up on the mesa, should anybody be watching. There were no other vehicles on the road, and when we were directly south of my house on the mesa, I told Amber to stop the car, leave the engine idling. Soon Jamie opened the side door and got in. He held his backpack on his knees. There was no reason to peel out, but the sand covered the highway and in her excitement Amber stepped on the gas too hard and burned rubber getting back on the highway. After a short time she turned on the car's headlights.

"Lemme drive," Jamie said. "You're going to get us pulled over."

"Shut up," Amber said.

31

"Stop for my board, okay?" Jamie said.

"You bet," I said.

"You can't hitchhike with a board," Amber said.

"I'm not going south without it," Jamie said. "Swell's building."

Far off in the distance you could see waves breaking white against the unseen pilings of the pier. We'd often stored our boards in Greg Scott's garage so we could walk to the pier after school let out, because the waves there were usually better than the beach break at Playa Chica. Sandbars would form around the structure, making for reeflike surfing.

And that big south swell was heading to the coast of California, the result of the hurricane off Hawai'i. The waves from the storm would hit our coast anytime, so the surf forecasters had said. Everybody who surfed was pumped up, waiting for the action. It looked as if Jamie would be getting those waves, while I wouldn't

I felt somewhat guilty for taking my mother's car — opening the garage and pushing it down the road before starting it, and without her permission — and definitely felt guilt for stealing all the cash in her purse. Yet there was an excitement in the air, a veiled electricity, what with the approaching big swell and the chaos surrounding Amber's and Jamie's lives.

Downtown was deserted, and we didn't want to get pulled over. For no reason the police would stop a car with kids in it late at night, and if they were looking for Jamie, well, they'd find him. Amber had her license so we were legal. Still, I was relieved when she turned on Ninth Street and got off the Coast Highway, heading toward Greg Scott's house. She coasted to a stop one house away from where our boards were stored.

The air was humid and thick with salt these few blocks up from the water. Palm fronds riffled above us as we made our way to the backyard. Even the streetlights seemed to conspire a sort of "muffled" light, if that's possible. You could hear the soft creaking of a nearby oil well, a remnant of the city's past, moving up and down, up and down, a mechanical beast of burden that never slept, so nobody would be able to hear any noise when Jamie got his board.

Amber and I went with him into the backyard. There was a sticky gate latch, which stuck, of course, and Jamie made a big *thunk!* muscling the gate open. The whole scene struck us as funny, and we began giggling, the first light moment since the beach this morning. Trying to suppress our laughter, we made our way to the garage. Inside, Jamie moved some boards, and Amber took hers, then I grabbed mine so that Jamie could get his, but a strange thing happened. Amber and I held on to our boards, leaving the backyard with Jamie. I don't think it was a conscious decision or anything, just an opportunistic moment of self-delusion.

"We need to get them back anyway," I whispered to Amber.

"Oh, absolutely." She nodded agreement.

As we loaded the boards in the back of the SUV I said, "Maybe we'll catch a few waves in the morning." It wasn't that far off.

"It might be good," Jamie said.

"Yeah," Amber said.

Suddenly Greg Scott showed up in the street. "What's up?" he said.

"Jamie's got to get away for a while," I said.

He looked at my mother's car. "Where you headed?"

"South," Jamie said.

"Do you have any stuff?" Greg Scott said.

"Just what's in my pack," Jamie said.

Greg Scott looked at all of us. "Hang on."

In a while he returned, carrying a pile of things. "This might help," he said, dropping it on the floor. Sleeping bags and towels and God knew what else. As he handed Jamie some money, he said, "Late." He turned and walked away.

Greg Scott was the best! Jamie, Amber, and I stood alone in the dark quiet street. We transferred the pile from the grass on the parkway into the back of the truck, trying not to make noise with the doors.

Avoiding Main, Amber drove the backstreets of town. When we were past the trailer park, we got on the Coast Highway, heading south, my mom's 4Runner our raft, the Pacific our Mississippi.

CHAPTER 4

The early morning swells humped on the horizon, racing toward shore. Once they hit shallow water the tops cascaded down and over each other with a lovely creamy-white grace, a turbulence contrasting with the still blue of the lightening sky and the deeper black-blue of the water.

I pulled myself out of the passenger side of the car. Amber was scrunched up though comfortable-looking in the back, a sleeping bag over her and her hand right on her mouth. Jamie was in the water, I supposed, for his board was gone — mine and Amber's were still underneath the car, safe and undisturbed — and I could see a surfer paddling through the swells.

Last night we'd driven until we could no longer stay awake, and we'd parked not far from the parking lot at Swami's, the nickname for the Self-Realization Fellowship grounds overlooking the reef break south of Encinitas.

Sometime before light, when I was groggy and Amber was out, Jamie drove us into the parking lot. The lot had a curfew posted, and we didn't want to get hassled by cops for something that dumb. Light was just dusting the golden dome of the temple. My mother's car was the only one in the lot.

As I pissed in the bushes I watched the surfer. Jamie, I could tell by the way he paddled. We'd surfed together since the summer of the fifth grade.

The summer after her husband's death Mrs. Watkins spoke to my parents about surfing. They all decided that it would be a good idea for Jamie and I to get boards. At that time Amber was going the cheerleader route, sneaking out of her bedroom window at night and running with the wild girls. She had no interest in surfing during that era. She did take it up when she was in the ninth grade, probably to impress Robert Bonham, who surfed really well. And when she started surfing she hit it with a vengeance.

So my parents and Mrs. Watkins took us to the beach a few times a week that summer and Jamie and I began our surfing lives. For Jamie it was a way to grieve, I guess, because he used to cry in the water sometimes. He thought nobody could tell, but I could. I let him have it, and was just there with him, just was with him.

We surfed and we shot hoops and we hung together, and even Amber got tired of hanging out with angry chicks who got in trouble all the time. It wasn't in Amber to be a criminal, like her screwed-up so-called friends of that time.

I looked back in the car; Amber showed no sign of waking so I was stuck — I couldn't leave her like this, asleep in a parking lot. "Ah," I sighed, looking over the ocean, wondering about Nestor and my mother. I could barely make out Jamie's form out in the water.

The summer between the seventh and eighth grades, our third full summer surfing, Jamie bestowed "best surfer" title on me. That summer his mother had worked out of necessity — it was after Mr. Watkins's death and before she married F — and on her way to work she dropped us off at the bluffs, where the waves were always better than in front of the mesa where we lived. This also saved us from having to ride our bikes on a two-lane road, pulling the board rack that Nestor had fashioned out of an old wagon for me.

That summer there was a sandbar buildup not far from the limestone cliff, which offered a great left. Jamie was goofy foot, meaning he faced the wave when going left; I was regular foot — I faced the wave when going right. On the prevailing south swells I became excellent at going backside, left, going with my back to the wave. I could crouch with one knee up and the other knee almost resting on the board and grab the outside rail, leaning into the wave, making ones that I shouldn't have, perfecting this maneuver while surfing the left-breaking sandbar all summer.

In mid-August, Claire Watkins stopped at the bluffs to drop us off, as she'd done many other workdays. It was a misty morning, not too unusual right along the coast, but the parking lot was filled with cars, and the entire cliffs were lined with onlookers, something we'd not seen any other summer day. Mrs. Watkins got out of her car with us. What we saw on the ocean that morning was a surfer's dream: summer morning south swell, huge empty waves. The biggest waves we'd ever seen. Not even the older surfers ventured out, and everyone stood hypnotized and in awe of the beautiful and violent display before them.

"You boys don't have to stay," Mrs. Watkins said, sensing our fear, our survival instinct, which was palpable. "I'll take you home. I've got the time, I'm early."

But Jamie and I knew we couldn't leave the beach, even though we probably wouldn't go out in the water. We just had to stay and watch, if nothing else.

Before she left, Mrs. Watkins extracted a promise from us that we would *not* go out in the huge waves. Only if it got smaller could we venture out. She wanted to force us to return home, but she knew that should we leave, we couldn't face any of the other boys who stood on the cliffs. Claire Watkins was cool that way, sensing subtle things that other parents didn't have a clue about. She didn't want to leave us, but she also didn't want to make us look foolish. So she went to work as she'd done countless other days that summer.

After she left, Jamie and I walked down to the beach with our boards and placed the towels and lunches in the sand as we always did upon arriving. The cliffs above us had a better vantage point for seeing the overall view of the waves marching to shore. Yet on the beach we had a better perspective of the size of the waves at water level. It was hard to judge size accurately since nobody was surfing, but we figured the waves were three to four feet overhead. Ten feet on the face? Usually the waves we surfed were two to four feet, once in a blue moon six feet on a big swell. These waves were the equivalent of Hawai'i's winter North Shore, surfing Mecca.

Plopping on the sand and not even bothering to remove our sweatshirts and short pants, we watched the incredible display of power all through the morning. Neither of us had any intention of going out in the massive waves, though we did begin taunting each other about doing so, since nothing was at stake because not even the older guys were going out.

So we sat, two thirteen-year-old boys on the beach. And watched. Like everyone else.

Until an older guy actually paddled out. He timed it in between sets, making it look relatively easy. He took off on the first wave of a set, and rode a huge blue beautiful peak all the way into the shorebreak, where he kicked out. Everybody on the clifftop yelled their approval. And soon more older guys were on the beach, waxing their boards before paddling out.

It wasn't crowded or anything, far more observers than actual surfers, but with guys in the water, it actually looked appealing. Until a set would roar through, wreaking havoc on the surfers in the water.

I hadn't intended to fall victim to one of Jamie's taunts, but I did. Already Jamie was much larger than I was, but we were both just skinny kids then. Still, I overcompensated to let him know he couldn't get inside my head. So I began waxing my board, pretending I was going to paddle out. All the while taunting Jamie. "You're such a woman," I said.

"At least I'm not a chicken shit bitch like you," he shot back.

"Who's waxing up? Not you, pussy." That got him in motion.

And on and on it went.

Before we knew what had happened we were both paddling for all we were worth to make it out over the massive shorebreak, the inside waves that were larger than anything we'd ever surfed. And, still, we paddled to make it beyond them and out into deeper water where the really large waves were.

Taking more than a half hour to make it outside, I knew that the only way in now was to catch a wave. Unless I totally chickened out and paddled back in before the huge crowd, which I wasn't prepared to do.

Thus we began making our way south toward the sandbar, though much farther out. I had never before been in such a disorienting mess! Just to maintain my position I had to paddle full out. Like paddling against a river. To make headway against the current I paddled like hell, and all the while the swells lifted me up and then set me back down, my stomach fluttering with each drop. Swells that weren't even close to breaking!

As I paddled south I broke from the pack of guys who were surfing directly in front of the bluffs, where Jamie had the good sense to remain. When a particularly huge set approached I found myself all alone trying to get out over the waves. I blasted through the last wave of the set, almost getting pulled back over the falls by the wave's momentum. My heart was *in* my throat. I had never before been so scared, thinking I was going to die.

Get it over with quickly! was my thought as I took off on the first wave of the next set. Jamie was north of me, hanging with the older guys, a much smarter move. I figured I would catch the wave, get crunched taking the drop, and then get pushed into shore by the rest of the waves, where I would be alive. I'd get creamed, but I'd survive. My heart was racing as I paddled to catch the wave that would save my life, or so I reasoned, because no sane thought could rationalize my even being on the ocean in these waves. I was lifted up, up, and then the bottom fell out, but I was on my feet on the board and my arms were straight up over my head and I'd made the drop! I cranked a backside bottom turn just like Kelly, then leaned forward, trimming my board, crouched, and tucked into the slot of the beast. I got tubed for a second and shot out on the shoulder of the wave and flew over its back and into freedom and immortality. The older guys in the water howled and yelled, and when I looked up onto the cliff I could see the gallery pumping their fists, though I couldn't hear their shouts. I had goose bumps, and felt queasy from all the adrenaline but the strangest thing was that I was no longer afraid. I wanted more and bigger waves. So I paddled back out.

Unfortunately for Jamie the later waves in the set are usually the bigger ones. He took off on the last wave and didn't make the drop. Later he told me that he didn't want to look like a wuss after I had gotten such a good ride. Jamie went straight down on the wave, his board's nose going directly into the water, buried until it was just too buoyant and then it launched itself straight back up into him. He'd made it to the surface and just as he was taking a huge gulp of air his board bumped his head a second time, closed his mouth with such force that all his front teeth were chipped (the doctor said that had his tongue been in the way it would have been cut off!).

As I got closer to him I could tell that he was in a daze. He wouldn't respond or anything. Another older and really good surfer was right there with me. He helped Jamie onto his board, even held on to him and the board through whitewater while I dove for the bottom.

"Can you get him in?" the older guy said.

"Yeah," I said. I undid my leash and let my board fend for itself.

Jamie just looked at me and the other surfer as if he were stupid; he wouldn't say anything.

"Let the whitewater push you in," the older guy said to me as we were hit by an incoming wave. I had a death grip on Jamie, and even with the initial blast of the wave, I held on to him and guided him into shore and safety.

Somebody on the bluff must have called the lifeguards, for there was a Jeep on the beach and a lifeguard took Jamie from me in shallow water. He lay Jamie flat on the sand. I told him that Jamie's board had hit him on the head.

Lifeguard: "What day is it?"

Jamie: "July."

The lifeguard then looked in Jamie's eyes. "His pupils are dilated." He looked in his ears. "No blood, so that's good. I'm going to call an ambulance. He needs to be checked out by doctors."

We were soon surrounded by other surfers and beachgoers. Some of the guys told me that I'd done really well. Jamie became sort of famous for getting whacked in really big surf. But he remembered that it was I who had surfed and surfed well, it was I who had brought him in. Still, it was the day that James Watkins left the beach in an ambulance.

He couldn't surf anymore that summer, and when I rode my bike back down to the cliffs a week later (Claire wouldn't drop me off, she'd never take us to the beach again), I was treated with deference and respect by the older guys. When school started, everyone knew of the event, and Jamie bestowed the title of "best surfer" on me. It had worked because Jamie, of course, was really the best surfer. It had been cool for a time.

Now, no sunlight shone on the ocean and it was dark down there, the surfer a black shape on top of the water. He reached far forward with every stroke, Jamie's stroke, as he made for the lineup where he could catch a wave. I wasn't sure how long Jamie'd been in the water — he'd been known to surf at night, if the waves held, even though nobody else could see a thing. "You don't need to see," Jamie would say. "You can *feel* the wave."

I watched the ocean, and watched Jamie ride a set wave as I walked back to the car. I knew I should be worried about what I had done, but wasn't. I wanted to get in the water! Yet Amber showed no signs of waking.

By the grace of God some locals came, making a bunch of noise, waking her. She seemed disoriented at first but when she saw me she smiled a big smile and then stretched slowly and luxuriously, all the time looking at me.

I nonchalantly took our boards from underneath the car; the locals checked me out, not saying anything, mostly looking at our boards.

"Wow," Amber said in her deep voice, which was deeper from sleep. She was brushing out her long hair so that it looked silky in the fresh morning light. When finished she rustled through her Hello Kitty backpack, pulling out a Strawberry something bag from which she took a small mirror. With her ring finger she patted some lotion on the fleshy part under her eyes. Then she just stared at me.

"What?"

"I can't believe what's going on. I can't believe what we're doing."

I couldn't either, so I changed the subject. "I'll go with you to a McDonald's or something."

Amber bared her teeth in front of the mirror and then looked out at the guys in the parking lot, and appreciated my chivalry, I hoped, because I really wanted to get in the water. There was no other choice when you traveled with a girl, I figured.

"Okay," she said, zipping the backpack. "How long's Jamie been out?"

"I don't know," I said.

"Thanks for staying with me, Juan," she said, and it sounded as if she meant it.

While Amber was in the restroom I bought orange juice. I looked outside for a pay phone, even walked over to a gas station next door, but there wasn't one around. When I got back to the car she was wearing a T-shirt over her bikini top, sitting in the front seat. I handed her the juice. She took a large gulp, spilling some on her shirt.

"Shit," she said.

When we returned there were more cars in the parking lot, though it wasn't yet crowded for the building swell. But it was a Monday morning, a school day, and September. Still, it was really odd that it wasn't more crowded, and word would travel quickly about the good waves that were lining up far outside at this fun break — hell, the damn surfcams would let everyone see! Now, the tide was dropping, the swell was increasing, and there were few surfers in the water. We took our boards from the back of my mother's car and waxed them on the grass that overlooked the parking lot. Again, the new arrivals checked us out, but we just went about our business.

Had I gotten out of the car alone, I would have been checked out and vibed out as well, probably. But with Amber it was different. They were checking her out as a girl more so than a surfer. Wait till she got in the water. She had Jamie's fearlessness, though wasn't yet up to his technical ability. She was improving, her confidence growing.

Descending the stairs to the sand, I counted the waves in a set. The horizon where the sky and ocean connected was a wavy mass of ripples, another indication of a swell. And the full force of the hurricane's waves wasn't supposed to hit the coastline for two days!

The shorebreak was large, making Amber somewhat restive as we waited for a lull in the waves to try to get out into the channel. We'd walked down the beach a good way so that we wouldn't have to paddle out through the whitewater of the breaking waves, a luxury you had when surfing a reef break.

To lighten up things, I ran into the water, gliding on my board for a time, and when a large shorebreak wave approached I paddled hard and stood up and jumped over the back of the wave, flopping in the cool sea.

"You're a fool," Amber yelled as she passed me by. She hadn't gotten wet getting through the shorebreak.

My trick had worked, however. Amber now paddled out, so I too began the long paddle out toward the break. The sun felt good on my back, heating the black wetsuit. Beyond the shorebreak the surface, as the depth increased, became a mysterious blue-black. Soft riffles on top of the water showed the path of the rip current as it headed back out to sea, where it had come from. Water in, water out. Eternally.

Some other surfers were behind us, paddling out. Suddenly Jamie took off far back in a breaking wave, dropping in and climbing up and down the face of the wave until it walled up in the shallow water. He trimmed his board, crouched, and blasted through the foam that hit his body and would have knocked off a less balanced surfer. Amber and I shouted encouragement to him as he continued on the wave, passing us, heading in toward shore. He backturned and pumped his board up and down into the shorebreak, then kicked out. "Yeah!" he shouted.

Amber and I raced to the lineup in the hopes of catching one of the waves of this set; I'd not yet timed the sets, so didn't know how long a wait we'd have between them — get it while you can! She took off on a nice little four-foot wave as the peak feathered over. I lost sight of her as she took the drop, then saw her again as she climbed the face of the small but well-formed wave. Once back up by the curl, she was again lost from my sight as she banked off the top and took the drop again. I watched her as the wave raced in to shore, watched her working the wave the same way Jamie had, trimming, casually withstanding the whitewater hitting her. When she came out of the whitewater she sometimes fiddled with her wetsuit because the bathing-suit straps would move on her shoulders. She did this in the same nonchalant way that some surfers grabbed their nose, or ran their hands through their hair, after making a wave.

I was comfortable. I was happy. Salt-smell permeates everything. The world is wet. Hump on the horizon heading toward you. Hump moving faster as it passes underneath your board. Your board moving as fast as you can get it to go with only your arms for oars —

like a sprinter ending the hundred-yard dash — and there's a second, a moment frozen in eternity, when you're not going forward and you're not going down the face of the wave, just before you take the drop, that moment when you are weightless, and everything is frozen, time has stopped, and that's the moment, I swear! The bigger the wave, the more intense the weightless time, the more your existence MEANS something. Out of existence, back in existence. The board flies over the surface of the wave, moving at its own speed times the speed of the wave moving in toward shore. On top of the wave, at the bottom of the wave, in the trough, moving toward the coastline at the speed of the wave. Ride up the face to the crest, whip the board back down the face to the bottom, each time somewhat weightless, though never as intense as the initial drop when you enter wavetime. Over and over you do this, until the wave closes out in the shorebreak, and you kick out, or do a floater wipeout, or jump off your board out the back of the wave, because it just doesn't matter; it's a blast!

After I kicked out I hustled to catch them. Jamie was slowly paddling out toward the lineup, Amber was paddling faster to catch him, and I sprinted to catch them both. One of the reasons you surfed with friends: so you'll have someone to talk to while paddling out, or while waiting for waves, or when revisiting the waves you'd just ridden.

"Did you see me get air?" Jamie said.

"Did you see my snapback?" Amber said.

"Did you see my floater?" I said.

We discussed our waves as we paddled back out into the lineup. Now, however, there were many other guys waiting for waves, guys who lived here, and who would have to share "their" surf with us. They *would* share, no doubt about it. Because surfing is all about what you can do. Not what you talk about doing, but what you actually do on the wave. And theoretically the guy who takes off closest to the curl of the wave, the position that is the most precarious, has the right of way. Jamie would take off as far back as possible, and so would I, and Amber could hold her own with these guys, I felt sure. Things could get tense if the proper rotation wasn't adhered to. In other words, if any guy from a group dropped in on members from another group, wild things could happen. I'd kicked out on a guy who'd dropped in on me. I'd seen Jamie launch his board just inches from a guy who'd snaked him. I'd seen him actually nail a guy with his board, a guy who'd had the audacity to snake him twice. I wouldn't drop-in on Jamie. He was six feet two inches tall, not one ounce of flab on him, and his lip was fat and his eye a little swollen from his fight with F. There were welts on his face and upper body. His nose was kinda big anyway, and now it seemed swollen, probably broken from F's punches on the beach yesterday. Jamie looked like a criminal, and maybe was one, for all I knew. Maybe he'd really injured F.

The tension was lessened when we got out to the lineup and one of the guys sitting on his board said to Jamie, "Excellent."

Jamie was the kind of surfer who inspired respect, appreciation, even, he was so good, his surfing special, rather than the competition a less accomplished though good wave rider attracted. He could be sponsored, if he wanted. If he'd enter contests. But he wouldn't. He said contests are pure bullshit. Contests have nothing to do with surfing, Jamie said. They're the opposite of what surfing is about, he said. Our high school surf coach said there was a spot on the team for Jamie. But Jamie said he wasn't a performing monkey, that surfing for him was a spiritual thing, and he wouldn't cheapen it by competing. The surf coach said no more.

Because of that dude's comment, when the next set came we held back, letting those guys catch the first waves, since we'd already had rides, and a nice rotation was established, one which worked until it was too crowded for any order, and by then the wind began to pick up. It started out as a riffle, tiny puffs of wind skirting the smooth surface but increasing steadily, the way the sun makes for the low horizon at sunset with the tenacity of a slow-moving tortoise. Soon the waves toppled over in an uneven fashion, and then the wind rippled the waves' faces, making for a bumpy ride. That, coupled with all the surfers in the water, and we knew the best part of the day for surfing was over. The strong west wind made the waves unmakeable, finally, and it was no longer fun.

Besides, I was tired and hungry and cold, what with the big chop that covered the horizon, making whitecaps out to sea. Kelp beds just beyond the reef kept the waves rideable far longer than would have been possible at our beach break. Still, we'd surfed a number of hours, all morning, from what I could tell by the sun's position in the sky, and we'd surfed some good waves, though not as big as I hoped they would be.

By the time we got back to the parking lot at Swami's, it was relatively empty, our car one of the few remaining. Down below, the surfspot was blown out, the reason nobody else was around. As we toweled off I thought of my mother. A deep sinking feeling struck me right in the gut. I shouldn't have taken the car. Not in a strict sense. But shit was going down last night. True, right now, we'd just gotten out of the water after surfing fun waves all morning. At present, things didn't seem so crucial. But last night they had been. And Jamie was safe. I was thinking that I'd get in trouble, but when I explained the immediacy of the situation my parents might not punish me. My father would be very angry — you're not supposed to steal the car! Yet Jamie was still around, not arrested last night. And the bonus was I didn't have to be at school, either. The surf was only going to get bigger, as one large blown-out set of waves crashing on the reef indicated.

Still, in spite of the fun waves, there was a melancholy feeling among us, for we knew that a parting of the ways was inevitable. Jamie would have to do what he was going to do. I'd have to get my mother's car back. Amber could return with me.

Jamie and I changed out of our wetsuits using towels wrapped around our lower bodies to hide that which needed to be hidden. Amber put on a T-shirt so she could remove her stuff and then did the same thing with her towel hiding her lower body. After changing we were all standing in the stiff breeze, not knowing what to say, what was to come next.

"Can I use your cell?" I asked Amber. Everyone knew the inevitable was here now.

She laughed, crinkling her nose. "I didn't pay the bill and they cut off my service." She had spread out a bunch of shells on the hood of my mother's car, things she'd collected while Jamie and I had remained in the water.

"No problem," I said. I didn't want to talk with my mother anyway; I was just going to leave a message on our home machine. I rooted through her found objects: a seagull feather; soft, rounded green glass; sand dollars; and a chunk of abalone shell. Her usual shit.

Jamie said, "Well, I guess this is it."

I tried to smile. "What'll you do?"

"Keep heading south. Baja. The waves will get better and better."

Jamie was right. The farther south you went, the better the surf would be, for the hurricane-generated waves were coming from the south so they'd have less distance to travel, less chance to dissipate their energy. I looked at Amber and she looked as if she were going to tear up. She looked at me for just a second and then turned her gaze out to sea.

"I'm not going back," she said. "I can't go back either." She sort of puffed herself up, making her seem taller than she was after she made her statement.

Oh, great, I thought. If Jamie were going on alone, I might have had a chance to return. He could take care of himself. The brother and sister hitchhiking team seemed somehow pathetic to me, whereas Jamie going off on his own wasn't.

My stomach growled so I changed the subject, something I was good at. "Let's get something to eat. We'll figure things out." I knew a great sandwich place back up the road where you could get the best avocado and sprout sandwiches in the world.

The Nuevo Papagayo had an outside deck that faced Pacific Coast Highway, where we sat eating. Amber and I had ordered avocado-and-sprout sandwiches on that homemade wheat bread, Jamie a tuna-fish sandwich. When I heard that term I always thought it was redundant. Like salmon fish. Or trout fish. Or lobster crustacean. But then there's catfish. Yet cats are mammals.

Jamie also said things like "warsh" for "wash," which pissed off Amber. And "eyetalian" for "Italian." "You sound like an Oakie," Amber would tell him. "I am," Jamie would say. Their parents were originally from Oklahoma, and Mr. Watkins used to say things like that when he was trying to be funny.

Away from the water and not far off the highway, the afternoon was warm. We were sheltered from the wind, but could see the giant eucalyptus trees all around rustling about. We sat in silence, enjoying the afternoon sun and each other's company.

Remembering something funny known only to her, Amber smiled before turning her back on us, facing the sun. Before she turned away I noticed that her eyes had small bags under them and her hair looked thicker from the salt water.

Jamie looked really tired. His nose was fat at the bridge, and he had a mouse under his right eye. The skin was scraped off some of his knuckles.

"Well, Watkins, you sure fucked up this time," I said.

He looked deep into my face. "At least I'm not a car thief like you."

"Ha! You've never taken your mom's car . . ." Then I stopped because I remembered all the shit that went down yesterday was because he had taken F's car.

Amber turned back to face us, seemingly glowing from the warm sun.

Jamie sighed and looked out over the highway.

I felt so comfortable with them, felt so normal, I didn't want the moment to end. "Puntos would be unreal with the swell that's coming."

The edges of Jamie's eyes creased and he laughed his high laugh, the first time since he came out of the water yesterday.

"It would," Amber said, her cheeks breaking into a huge, knowing smile.

How did she know? She'd never been there. Puntos was my spot. It was a peak wave, breaking in shallow water over smooth rocks. It was just north of Ensenada, Baja California, Mexico. I'd surfed there on summer south swells, and nobody could touch me, not even Jamie. It was my power spot.

"My aunt has a place at San Rafael. Maybe Jamie could stay for a while." He would be safe there, and then Amber and I could return to get him when things cooled off at home. I was already in trouble, so one more day wouldn't matter, I figured, in the big scheme of things.

"Would you drive us down there, Juan? Could Jamie stay there?" Amber said in a voice that made me want to do anything for her.

"Yeah."

"You've already done plenty," Jamie said. "You should get back with the car."

"I want to ride some big waves," I said. "A perfect wave."

"Ha!" Jamie said.

There was another consideration as well. Should my parents report the car stolen, the police in Mexico probably wouldn't know about it. But in California, they sure would. So the sooner we got south, the better chance Jamie would have of steering clear of them. This was the bogus logic playing out in my mind. In reality, I didn't want to look like a wuss in front of Amber. Plus I didn't want to be in school; I'd rather surf big waves than waste my time being bored. And this: I didn't want my friend cast adrift to suffer his fate solo. We could be together for a time, maybe see him settled at my aunt's trailer, till it was cool for his return.

We repacked the car, loading the boards on top so that when we crossed the border there would be no doubt about our intent.

"You drive, Amber," I said as we climbed into my mother's 4Runner. She'd disarm the Federales at the border.

With the afternoon warmth permeating the car, and the wind rustling through the open windows as we headed south, Jamie softly snored.

CHAPTER 5

"Dog meat tacos."

"Jamie!" Amber said.

Laughing, I spat out the bite I had just taken. I could see some dogs lying in the sun by my mother's car, a thin pit bull and a wiry German shepherd mix, sniffing their genitalia, scratching their backs by snaking upside down on the dirt.

It was a hot afternoon, yet in spite of the heat I could smell the smoke from wood-burning fires, smell food being cooked, tacos and churros, and once in awhile smell the fetid stench of raw sewage as it wafted up the streets from the river. We stood on Avenida Revolución in Tijuana, Mexico! in plain sight of the car — I'd heard all the stories about thefts when in TJ — and had paid a boy to watch it. For a dollar, he said he'd protect our car. Since he was probably the thief, Jamie had said, it would be in our best interest to pay.

My mother's 4Runner was down an incline on a dirt track that led to some shacks, just off the main drag. The boy smiled and waved to me as I memorized where we were: Revolución and Second. Not too far from a big arch that was like photos I'd seen of the gateway to St. Louis.

"No, really," Jamie said, "they make these tacos out of dog." He hiccupped a few high laughs.

"Would you stop," Amber said.

I didn't care what they were made of, they were delicious.

There was something about the way the tacos were prepared right in the open, right on the street, the fire before you in a rolling cart, and the cook/vendor so eager to please, his movements quick and assured. What Jamie said about dog meat was the standard rap against Tijuana. It was a poor town, a town next to a rich city, San Diego, and the U.S. Navy was stationed there to boot. Always there were sailors crossing the border, spending their money. Supposedly anything went. Strip shows and whorehouses. But I'd never been here at night. Thus far it didn't seem so bad. And this: I'd only driven on the outskirts of town on my way south with my parents during summers when we'd stay as a family at my aunt's trailer on the beach in Baja California. Mexico, with its blaring poverty and wild art and tumultuous history, felt like home to me. And it was, on some level.

Yet you're still crossing a border, aware that you're entering another country. That's obvious. But the change, the border, is so stark, so striking, so breathtaking in its contrast, that it's almost stunning if you think about it.

You drive the I-5, the American freeway, all the way to San Ysidro. While you're approaching you can see the hills of Tijuana in the background, looming up, getting more distinct with each passing mile: shacks and houses and villas with smoke curling up from maquiladora chimneys and house chimneys. A distinct contrast from the lush, developed hills of La Jolla, say, contrasted in their tired brown appearance, end-of-summer slumping from the persistent four months of heat already endured by its inhabitants.

As you actually cross the line of demarcation you can see to your left the orderly and repressive-looking archway where the American agents question anyone entering the U.S. from Mexico. On this side, the side entering Mexico, there are Federales in their khaki uniforms looking disinterested as you roll by. Then you're funneled into waves of traffic, emptying into a bustling and vibrant downtown, almost European, in your imagination at least. The whole transition takes a matter of minutes, but the feeling lasts, is profound, even, when you think back on it. Especially if you've taken your mother's car because your best friend has thrashed his so-called stepfather.

Now we were golden tired after surfing the good waves at Swami's, and it was a warm afternoon with the low sun glinting off buildings and tin roofs. Traffic sounds — horns honking, buses chugging forward emitting dark trumpets of smoke, ranchera music from passing cars — and food smells, along with bright objects for sale right on the sidewalk, assailed my senses. Street vendors and pharmacies and all sorts of specialty shops dotted the streets. The odd thing was how you'd be walking on a sidewalk next to a paved street and then, bam! no sidewalk, just dirt, and the street was suddenly rutted and dusty. Then there'd be a really nice store, along with food carts, and the street and sidewalk would reappear.

And there were strip joints, which Jamie seemed very interested in and which I masked my interest in for Amber's sake.

"I want to go to a bar," Jamie said.

"What for?" I said. "Let's get out of town." Even though I was now almost relaxed about having taken my mother's car since there were no American police here, I was excited and scared because I *had* taken my mother's car! We *were* in Tijuana! We had surfed the front edge of the approaching swell. And Jamie was okay, not arrested or anything. "We need to get to my aunt's." I wanted to say, Let's get some waves.

"I want to see if I can buy."

"Anybody can buy here, dunce." Amber was ahead of us, pigeon-toeing her way over the sudden dirt.

I looked at Amber and Jamie and couldn't control my excitement, doing a little shuffle with my feet.

Looking back at us, she shrugged her shoulders and made a face at Jamie.

I didn't resist, though I should have, and we now had a reason to wander the crowded streets in the time before dark but when it is no longer day. The strange thing was — what *hadn't* been strange in the last twenty-four hours? — a man on a skateboard followed us, it seemed. A man on a skateboard is somewhat unique in general, but this man was particularly striking since he rode his out of necessity. He had no legs. Cut off right where the legs meet the hips. He had a powerful upper body, and wore fraying gloves, which slightly protected his hands as he literally paddled over Tijuana's streets the way we paddled our boards over the ocean's water.

I'd first noticed him after we'd crossed a street on the light and he'd followed after it had changed, right through traffic, with cars honking and drivers yelling. It didn't seem to faze him. I don't know why he followed us, but he did, persistent as hell, always there. We'd go in a shop — Amber was looking for some long pants and maybe a light jacket, since she'd only brought her cut-off Levi's and my sweatshirt — and Half-man on Skateboard would be a few doors away, tailing us like a bad detective. He started to bother me, and I couldn't concentrate on anything else after a while. I didn't tell Jamie or Amber, figuring I'd wait and see what the guy wanted. Probably a handout, and I didn't blame him, and I would give him money, should he ask.

As we entered an alleylike outdoor shopping plaza, Amber said, "I like that skirt." She looked around at clothes while I looked at the statuary that was all over the floors. Carved frogs and busts of Indian-looking guys, and yard ornaments. Jamie gravitated to a big display case that had a bunch of switchblade knives.

"Here's a nice one for F." He pointed with his index finger toward a huge bowie knife. The edges were serrated and I could feel at that moment the hatred Jamie had toward F. It showed on his split and raw knuckles.

"I don't think so, Rambo."

"Hey, guys, what do you think of these?" Amber held some tapestry pants with a drawstring next to her Levi's cutoffs. She also held up a jacket — a tightly woven cotton Indian one that's warm when it's cold but cool when it's hot — a great jacket, a Baja jacket, blue and white and green with a hood on it.

I watched her pay the full price for the clothes; she hadn't even tried to bargain with the guy. "Amber, next time let me do the talking."

"Why?"

"'Cause I'll get you a better price. You don't pay the asking price. Everybody knows that."

"I don't want a bargain. If that's the price, then that's the price. These guys aren't rolling in dough, you know."

"Hey, Juan, get me a deal on that bowie knife. It's got F's name on it."

"You're not funny," Amber said, pulling on her jacket.

Most of the barkers outside strip joints left us alone as we passed, because we were with Amber, and there seemed to be a very strong sense of propriety toward an American girl. Yet there was also a strong sense of machismo too because the men couldn't help but stare at her. I, of course, was always aware of her sexuality because she was constantly in my life and I'd always had a crush on her, I think. But she was Jamie's sister, older than both of us, and that was that. I'd never seen the effect she had on men, however. Granted, the guys on the TJ streets were not pillars-of-the-community types, but they were men who could see the beauty of a woman, of that I was sure. And Amber was striking in that dusk as we made our way in the time when the streetlights haven't taken over. She wore her new clothes and she looked happy, for the moment at least, and we had forgotten, however temporarily, why we were there in the first place.

When finally we stood outside a bar that we all agreed seemed okay — American rock music blasted from Club City Light, and laughter and shouting emanated from within — I'd lost sight of Half-man on Skateboard, which was just as well, for I might have been unable to enjoy myself once inside.

Club City Light had a long polished bar in a large rectangular room. The cement floor was covered with sawdust and beyond was a raised dance floor toward the back. It was crowded, almost exclusively with Americans, many who'd been drinking all day judging by the loud whoops and frantic energy that hit you like a wet towel once inside. There were periodic rumbles of laughter and sound, vibrating the large mirror behind the bar. Three bartenders hustled behind that bar, spilling liquid, bumping into each other, and generally jamming to keep up with the consumption of the drunks.

Buying beer was not a problem. First Jamie bought a round, looking particularly tough with his battered face and aviator sunglasses on, even inside. Then I got one, and Amber did too as we stood in various places around the bar. I didn't much care for beer, but after three of them, I was feeling it. One summer when Jamie and Amber and Claire had gone to Oklahoma to visit their relatives and I was in Ensenada on a surfing trip with some older guys, I'd had gin and tonics at Hussong's Cantina. They had made me sick, but I figured I could stomach these beers. Yet Jamie showed no sign of slowing down. In fact, he began flirting with an older woman, someone who was at least twenty-five. Probably because she sat at a table. Her hair was up in a bun and she wore makeup and tight pants and a slingshot T-shirt that showed her chest.

All of a sudden I saw a guy who looked like Greg J. heading for the door. He was with some older guys. "Is that Greg J.?" I shouted.

"Where?" Jamie yelled back, taking his gaze off the woman.

Amber, while turning to look, bumped into my shoulder. By the time she was all the way around, the guy was gone.

Jamie said so the woman couldn't hear, "His dad's cool, but not that cool." He refocused his gaze on the woman.

"Ha!" I half-shouted. Jamie was right, Greg J.'s dad wasn't going to bring him to a bar in TJ, surf trip or no surf trip.

"It's packed," Jamie said.

"You can sit here," the woman said.

Jamie grinned huge, dwarfing that damn Cheshire cat. "Cool," he said, moving toward her

Jamie was changing fast. In two days he'd fought F and won, run away, and now was with a *woman*! When he was young he had been shy on land, but aggressive in the water. Always he would stand up for himself in the water, but not necessarily so on land. On land it had been a different deal. I guess things were changing for him pretty fast. Jamie was with a woman in a bar!

"Moo!" I bellowed as he sat on her lap. *Moo* was Jamie's name for old women, because of a sixth-grade science film that called cow teats "mammary glands."

"How old are you?" the woman said.

"Nineteen," Jamie said.

Amber almost spat out her drink of beer.

"Easy," I said.

She cracked up.

Maybe Jamie looked dangerous with his battered face, and maybe the people with whom the woman sat were so drunk they couldn't tell our ages. Who knew? Something happens to people when they cross the border; something exits the consciousness of otherwise reasonable people when they enter Mexico. Under normal circumstances the twenty-something-year-old woman probably won't ask the fifteen-year-old boy to sit on her lap — they quickly reversed the scene, with the woman standing so that she could sit on Jamie's lap — and have her friends make room for us at their table, a small wet affair. The woman and her friends ordered round after round of beers.

"Where you guys from?" one of the old men asked Amber after staring at her for ten hours.

"Nowhere, everywhere," I said, but he didn't hear me because he wasn't paying any attention to me.

They were from San Francisco and on vacation, I think they said through shouted snippets that I caught. Two couples and the woman, newly divorced. That was why they were here. The older guys gawked at Amber, and when they did it for too long, I howled the long coyote howl — *ahohh, ow, ow, ow.* Horn dogs all of them. Old guys, drunks in the bar, would come up and shout conversation to Amber.

Maybe that was why she began to cling to me, first holding my hand, and then draping her arm over my shoulder. Jamie, by then, was all over that woman, even making out with her. I had never seen such a thing, such a public display by him.

The border, I supposed. And we were all sort of drunk, so much so that Amber and I even began kissing. I couldn't believe it! I was making out with Amber. In a bar. Our inhibitions had been sufficiently lowered by alcohol and geography and events, I supposed, for the old social order was down. Gone. The very thing they warned us about in those propaganda films about the evils of alcohol and drugs. I could make out in public with Amber, something I'd always aspired to. Her lips were chapped but soft because of lip gloss, and her taste was sweet, somehow, in spite of the beer we'd drunk, and her soft creamy hair fell over my shoulder as we kissed. Yeah! I'd known her my whole life it seemed, and here we were drinking and making out in a bar in Mexico. Double yeah!

And time passed through a gauzy veil of shouted conversations coupled with the din of sluggish drunken movement. Jamie was hooked up with the woman, and I mostly thought of Amber instead of talking even though she was right next to me, was leaning on me, since it was too hard to talk, and, besides, Amber wasn't a talker in the best of times. But she'd yelled at me before. And had hit me, had hit me with one of her Hello Kitty backpacks. Right in the head.

I remembered when Jamie and I had been all over Red Vines for a time. We noticed that after eating some, when you spat, whatever you hit would be red. We thought that detail was pretty cool. What do you expect from fourth graders?

So we'd order Red Vines from Claire Watkins or my mother, load up on them, and spit on anything that moved or didn't move.

I don't even remember how it happened, but I accidentally spat Red Vine juice on Amber's white tennis shoes. Amber was in sixth grade and quick. That Hello Kitty backpack must have had twenty pounds of gear in it, the Strawberry Shortcake bag chock-full of makeup and lipstick and other girl paraphernalia, and she tagged me on the side of the head before my spit had even hit her shoe. I was stunned but tried to get away. She ran me down like a cowboy bulldogging a steer, rubbing my face in the their backyard grass.

As I now looked at her hair right in my eyes, I could smell it (ocean), and was almost mad thinking about how she had rubbed my face in the grass. I leaned forward, licking her ear in between all the piercings dangling like tiny Christmas ornaments, moving my way up to an ear cuff, where I chomped down. She *had* rubbed my face in the grass.

"Ow!" Amber shouted. "What's the matter with you?"

"Sorry, sorry."

She gave me a hard look and then went back to watching the woman with Jamie.

How could I get mad at her when I thought about how messed up the whole thing was after Mr. Watkins's accident? She was always strong, and willing to use her strength, as she'd done when she rubbed my face in the grass. I thought about how far she'd come after Mr. Watkins's death when she'd befriended the tough girls, girls who got in trouble at school smoking and drinking and fighting even. She was kicked off the cheering squad, but hadn't seemed to care.

But none of that shit was her true nature, and when the rowdy girls found out she was just posing, they turned on her, sort of. They stopped hanging with her, they stopped including her in their shoplifting sprees, stopped coming to get her to sneak out and drink on school nights.

Amber leaned forward, squinting at Jamie and the woman. I finished my beer, banishing Amber's transgressions against me, and looked at him too.

He frowned at Amber and me as he came toward us. Once close enough, he leaned down and said, "I'm outta here."

"No, you don't!" Amber said.

I was dumbfounded, but he was leaving, walking right out of the bar with that woman! What with all the drinking and with being drunk on Amber, I was mostly unaware of the implications of Jamie's departure, though I do remember the reflection off his sunglasses as he looked back at us before he walked out the door.

"That's just great!" Amber yelled through all the other shouts emanating from Club City Light.

"Moo!" I bellowed after Jamie. He flipped me the finger.

The two remaining couples simply stared at Amber and me. I stared back at the old men, howling a few times.

I didn't like the fact that we were separating. But I was glad for Jamie — that woman was good-looking. She oozed sexuality while prancing out of the bar with him.

With nothing to say to the people from San Francisco, and my periodic howling, Amber pulled me out of Club City Light.

Hand in hand and somewhat drunk, we began walking for the car. The streets were far less crowded, and it must have been after midnight, and Half-man on Skateboard was there, behind us, the wheels making a tiny echo in the damp street.

"That guy's creepy," Amber said, becoming aware of his presence.

I said nothing.

I'm not sure how we found the car, or how long it took us, but it must have been pretty late by then. I quickly opened the passenger-side door, letting Amber in. I then stood in the dirt street, just off the broken curb, waiting for Half-man on Skateboard. His passage was slowed, though not by much, over the hard-packed dirt. A thin beach overcast now dusted all the cars and every object around, giving the world a dull sheen. The man rolled up to Amber's window and stopped. This seemed to amuse her on some level, for she began laughing.

I wasn't amused; I was outside with the guy. His upper body was like the lower body of a regular person. His arms were like short legs, like Shetland pony legs, and his chest was made of iron. His face glistened with sweat. But he was oddly clean and well-groomed, as far as I could tell. Sort of like a minotaur, though without the bull's body.

He looked through the window at Amber for a time, and then turned his gaze upon me. His eyes were dark and piercing and his whole body seemed to vibrate with an otherworldliness. He said: "Beware your friend."

And then skated off into the night, swallowed up by the overcast like a heavenly apparition.

"What did he say?" Amber asked when I got in the car.

"I'm not sure," I said.

"I don't want to stay here," she said. She leaned against me.

We looked into each other's eyes and began kissing. When we came up for air I said, "What about Jamie?"

"Those people are staying at the El Conquistador. Can you find it?"

"You bet." The town wasn't that big. We could always get a tourist map, should it come to that.

"He can just wait there. We can get him in the morning." She leaned against my shoulder and promptly fell asleep.

I sat there thinking what an odd night. I'd wanted to be with

Amber forever, and here she was actually with me, and, still, everything was so strange, and the front of my face felt as if it weren't even there. I remembered looking at ancient Aztecan art and thinking, How could they create that stuff? It was so other-worldly, their art. That was what I felt sitting in my mother's car in the early hours of the misty Tijuana morning, water droplets on the windshield, obscuring my vision. It was as if we'd been transported to some other planet, an alternative world in which we still inhab-ited our earthly bodies, but those were the only remnants of the world we'd come from. Amber was with me. We were free of all pre-vious social constraints for the moment, which made me excited until I thought of my parents, and then the excitement was re-placed by dread. But I could feel Amber nestled into me, could feel her soft curves and her breath hot on my neck, and I was prepared to suffer the consequences for this moment.

Starting the car and slowly pulling forward, I drove to a beach south of town with Amber cooing in her drunken state, and we slept together in the back of the SUV, holding each other, and I think that she too had always desired me. She must have.

CHAPTER 6

Just below San Rafael, where the trailer park and houses were, below where my aunt had a trailer, was the surf spot called Puntas. The mesa simply stopped, and the cliff gave way to a miniature bay. Round rocks covered the beach, and they also formed a reef outside, the waves lining up in near-perfect peaks, both a right- and a left-breaking wave. Puntas was best with a healthy swell and a receding tide.

You can't see the waves breaking from the highway, but you can see the effects of the swell. Relentless lines moving toward the coast. Marching in a cosmic rhythm that God only knows, and that we were trying to tap into. Since there was a swell on this day, and it wasn't too late, we made for more surfing. Why not? We could go to my aunt's trailer after. I could drop off Jamie there, and if Amber and I drove fast, we could be back home before it was too late.

Driving off the paved highway and onto the dirt road that wound its way over the small mesa, a dust cloud followed our car as we made our way to the surf spot. There was a flat area to park and camp, and then a gully, and then a path down the cliff's face. We parked, stretched, and made our way to the mesa's edge. Except for the light wind that blew, Puntas was seemingly perfect. Tide dropping. Shoulder-to-head-high waves. Greg J. wasn't down here; we were getting the good waves, the hurricane swells!

"Yeah!" Jamie said. "Oh, my head."

"Moo," I whispered. My head hurt too. When we'd picked him up at El Conquistador, he looked sort of young and forlorn, waiting right at the entrance. Looking nothing like the player of the night before, he still wore his sunglasses, and he looked a little tough, but he also looked fifteen standing there on the Tijuana street in the early morning light. When he got in the car he smelled like vomit; it was kind of pathetic. Amber had said nothing. I too gave him some time before I tried to tease him about that woman. To his credit he wouldn't respond, wouldn't take the bait, had said nothing about his night. Probably because she had chosen him, not the other way around. Or she was an old lady or something. Who knew?

Amber hadn't mentioned last night either, but we were all dry-mouthed and grungy and weren't talking that much. Maybe she was embarrassed in front of Jamie, I don't know. Maybe she was apprehensive about surfing unknown waters. I know I was scared shitless the first time I'd surfed here.

"The rocks are rounded, and there's a channel to paddle out in. I've never seen a shark here." Last summer I surfed here every day for a week while my family stayed at my aunt's trailer. Jamie was with me, and the waves had been small but fun. Another time, I'd camped down here with some older guys. Actually at San Rafael, but we'd ended up surfing here because San Rafael was a one-man wave, and it easily became too crowded. I knew this place, knew it better than Jamie.

"There's nothing to be afraid of," he said, already changing right in front of us, using a towel.

"Moo," I said.

"Fuck off, Juan."

The Pacific Ocean in Mexico is the same one you encounter in California. But it *feels* differently because it's in another country. Maybe that was why Amber was hesitant, I don't know. But she was suddenly modest, an irony, because we'd held each other, and I hadn't slept for her closeness and my desire that had raged all night. Still, we'd not done it, though we'd explored each other's bodies with a luxurious sense of time, relishing the new sensations as if they'd last forever, as I knew they would.

I came out of my reverie, walked to the opposite side of the car from where Amber was, and began changing out of my pants. The waves were calling, there wasn't another soul at this very good surf spot, and it appeared that Amber now wanted some privacy.

"It's an easy paddle out, there's a channel," I said.

"Yeah," she said, suddenly unapproachable. I tried to watch her change but she gave me the knife-stare, so I took off down the path to the water.

Getting out into the lineup was slow going. The tide was out and the stones covering the inside were round and slick with a green moss. When it became deep enough to float my board I began paddling. You couldn't paddle very fast because you'd hit rocks and slip off your board in the light tidal surge inside. Even after it became deeper, every so often you could push off rocks with your hands, but nothing mattered — the sun was hot, and I was in Mexico with Jamie and Amber!

When it was deep enough I dunked myself in the cool refreshing ocean, drenching my aching head. I looked back and saw Amber maneuvering the cliffside. Once in the water she paddled too fast and hit a rock, slithering off her board. Not hurt or anything, she scrambled back on with a new awareness.

Out in the break we huddled together. From the mesa the waves had looked shoulder-high. Yet out here in the lineup, they were overhead. Puntas is so much fun because you can take the drop fading left, hit the bottom and crank a huge turn, and then climb up the face of the wave just ahead of the whitewater, and then bank off the lip with a snapback, and take the drop again. At low tide, as it was now, the lip of the wave throws out just a bit, just enough to make it fun, and with the added size, there was a little something at stake, though the waves were surprisingly gentle for how big they were getting. A perfect wave for Amber to ride. And the reason I loved it so much: its forgiving nature.

"This wave's cool, Amber," I said. "It's easy to make and the water's not that shallow."

"You can go either way," Jamie said.

"I'm fine, you guys," she said.

"I know," I said, taking off on the first set wave, bottom turning so that my right hand dragged in the water, and then was covered by the wave — tubed! sort of — without getting in the whitewater. The wave was well overhead, and I could hear both Jamie and Amber yelling encouragement as I nailed a huge cutback once outside the hollow part. With a peak wave the process of getting covered lasts for a very short time. That first wave was probably the best wave I'd ever ridden in my life — an omen, I just knew.

I watched Jamie and Amber take off on the same wave as I paddled back out. Jamie cranked an outrageous bottom turn and then flew up to the lip, where he snapped back and took the drop again. Amber just sort of angled her board right, made it past the first breaking whitewater of the peak, and then did a nice cutback followed by a smooth bottom turn, heading into the lineup in shallower water. She kicked out close to where I paddled and kept gliding on her board toward me. Then she dove forward, her body crossing right in front of me, first her head and then her rear and then her calves right before my eyes as she passed over and into the water. I dove forward, catching her from behind, and when we surfaced, we embraced, wetsuit to wetsuit in the warm sunny waves. Jamie yelled something, but he was too far away to hear, though I had an idea.

"Is Jamie going to get all weird on us?" I said.

"What's to get weird about?" Amber said. "We're not doing anything wrong." She kissed me, untangled our leashes, and got on her board and paddled back out into the lineup.

I followed her, thinking no, I hadn't done anything wrong. I wasn't supposed to be in school right now or anything, and Nestor was probably going to give me a reward or something when we got back. Ah, give it up, I thought, as the excitement of Amber and the energy of the waves took over my consciousness.

On another ride I was tubed in the walled-up shorebreak. I raised my arms in triumph, but neither Amber or Jamie had seen the wave — Jamie was paddling far beyond what had been the takeoff point for a particularly large set that was approaching, and Amber was getting back on her board in the trough between the breaking waves and where the shorebreak formed.

I'd never seen Puntas close out — get so big that the wave loses its shape — but the wave Jamie caught was as near to closing out without doing so as it could be. He took the huge drop, the face of the wave almost twice as tall as he was, and carved a fluid bottom turn heading left, his only mistake. It appeared that the water was deeper in the south end of the bay, the wave's lip holding up much longer for a rider who would have gone right. Once Jamie trimmed his board on the wave of the day, you could see that it really was no longer a peak. The left, the way Jamie rode, was a huge uneven wall of water with no way for him to make the wave. It engulfed him with no mercy, spitting his board in the air. Jamie surfaced, hollered, and got back on his board

"I'm going in," I yelled to Amber.

She agreed, and caught a shorebreak wave in. I caught a wave in too. Soon we were both back in shallow water, doing the careful dance through the mossy rocks to get in without breaking an ankle.

It had been afternoon by the time we'd arrived, and the wind had picked up into a steady breeze, which made the relatively unprotected waves bumpy. This fact, along with a rising tide, made for mushy waves, ones that were no longer fun. We dried off in the sun, and for the first time I thought about our next move.

"All right," I said.

Jamie looked at me.

"Where to now?" Amber said.

"My aunt's trailer."

"Do you have a key?" she said, pulling on her new pants.

"It's not hard to get in." Once when my father forgot our key, he'd jimmied a window and I had crawled in, then opened the door. I could do it again, though it might be dicey if the owners of the trailer park were around. As we loaded our things for the short ride back up the coast, I said, "It'll work out."

Of course it didn't. The guard gate where you check in was unoccupied, which I'd planned on, but I hadn't figured that someone would be *in* my aunt's trailer. Someone else staying there.

We idled by, dumbstruck that a car was in front, music playing, people walking around inside. Not my aunt and uncle.

"What the?" I said.

"The best laid plans . . . ," Amber said.

Jamie just laughed. "No problem."

I parked the car, and we sat there maybe fifteen minutes, flummoxed and tired, not knowing what the next move should be.

Amber solved the problem by saying, "I need some things from a store."

CHAPTER 7

The road to Ensenada curves back into a valley and then heads toward the coast once again, opening on a broad horizon that shows all of Bahia de Todos Santos. You get a similar vista when you come upon San Rafael, though that view gives you the entire picture, while the view right before the city of Ensenada shows you a microcosm of the same bay. Ensenada is a fishing town, formerly a village. I like to think of it as a century behind Los Angeles in terms of population, and geographically it's a mirror image of Los Angeles, though much smaller. On land it's surrounded by mountains, and one of its borders is the sea, as in Los Angeles.

The first thing you notice when the vista opens over the city is the harbor. It's not huge, though there are plenty of fishing boats in dry-dock in various stages of construction, and there are sometimes a few ships — party boats that ply the Pacific coastline between Los Angeles and Acapulco.

Jamie drove us into the small city, our thoughts focused on getting a good meal; we were hungry after surfing, and sort of befuddled because of the presence of people at my aunt's trailer. My plan hadn't counted on that. And I was trying to hide my nervousness, my anxiety about what we were doing; Jamie and Amber were just in the moment, I guess, because they hadn't stolen their mother's car. Though technically Jamie had stolen Claire Watkins's car hundreds of times, had "stolen" F's car two mornings ago, getting us to this point.

After parking right on the main drag in front of a restaurant called Bahia de Ensenada (we just had to eat!), we entered the place where they had the best seafood. I ordered *pescado ranchero,* which is a dish consisting of chunks of fresh fish in a ranchera sauce — chile, onions, tomatoes, and cilantro. Jamie ordered a taco platter, and Amber had chicken *mole,* a dark brown sauce made from chile, chocolate, nuts, and spices. My favorite aspect of the Bahia de Ensenada restaurant was the glass-enclosed cooking area next to the cash register where women hand-made tortillas. They were thick and fresh and retained the smoky flavor of the wood fire they were cooked over. Jamie and I sipped our cold sodas as we waited for the food. Amber went to use the restroom.

As Jamie hunkered over the small table, he said, "Nestor likes this place, right?"

"Yeah, he does." He'd brought us here when Jamie stayed with my family on our vacation. Jamie's face was getting red from the sun and wind. His nose was still pretty swollen, and he kept his sunglasses on to help hide the marks on his cheek and under his eye.

Amber made her way back to the table, holding a wad in her hand.

"What do you have?" I said, pointing to the paper towel.

"I just washed some stuff."

When she sat in her chair, her leg touched mine. I didn't move my leg, and she didn't either. "We should have just gone to the police." A little late for rational action, I thought.

"Are you kidding?" Amber said.

"And get arrested?" Jamie said.

"Assault, it's called." I took a crispy tortilla chip and dipped it in the *salsa fresca*.

"I won. He said he'd charge me with battery."

"You guys are witnesses, right? Your mother saw it."

"She won't go against him," Amber said.

"Why not?"

"It's like he has some power over her or something. That, and the fact she's embarrassed she married the jerk slob."

"No shit. That's why I'm not going back," Jamie said. "Ever."

"We'll set you up here. We'll come back when things are cool."

"No, it's over for me there. I'm going to kill F next time I'm around him. I wanted to kill him when I was bashing his head on the floor. If I get the chance, I'll just kill him. I'm not angry or upset or anything. That's just a statement of fact. The next step in our relationship. I'm going to kill him. I've decided. If I go back it's gonna be to off him."

"Dude, going postal?"

A waiter appeared with an oversized tray that had all our food on it. My appetite had sort of dimmed by what Jamie was saying, but I did my best to eat the good food that was placed before me.

"You're not killing anybody, Jamie," Amber said.

"I will. The world will be a better place without him." Jamie took a big bite from his taco.

"Look, player, I didn't go through all this shit so you'd be locked."

Jamie calmly folded his hands and placed them on the edge of the table. "You don't know F." He gave Amber a stare of shared knowledge. Her lips parted ever so slightly as she gazed upon him.

"I'm in deep shit, Scarface. Because of you. You have to stay out of trouble. You owe me."

"It's really been tough on you, hasn't it, Juan?" Jamie put the taco back on the plate. "Those waves have been nasty to you."

Amber couldn't keep a straight face and began laughing. So did Jamie. Me too.

❦

On the outskirts of town we found *Gigante*. While Amber and I went in, Jamie waited in the car. I could translate if Amber couldn't understand something.

But on the way in I noticed there was a bank of pay phones to the right of the main entrance. As we neared them I hesitated.

"What's up?" Amber said.

"I'll be there in a minute, okay?"

She looked at me, then past me, seeing the phones. "Yeah, no problem."

I turned and faced my fate. I had heard all kinds of crap about how bad the phones are in Mexico but I got an operator right away. It did take some time for the line to get through, though. And when it did and our phone machine answered, I told the operator my parents were screening, someone would accept the call after the beep sounded. When the beep did go off, I shouted "I'm okay!" before the operator cut the line since I was calling collect. Of course the opera-

80

tor *did* hang up on me. But my parents would have heard me, known my voice, I was sure of that. The phone machine had picked up.

Inside I caught up with Amber, who was strolling along, looking at all the odd Mexican items. Still not acknowledging our actions of the previous night, we walked through the market, where we saw *nopalitos,* rows of canned jalapeños, sweet bread — *pan dulce* — and candles in large glass jars with the pictures of saints on them. Not to mention just the regular items such as napkins and tissues and cereals, which had their packaging in Spanish, of course. We hustled right through the meat section, which had the tangy smell of blood about it. After wandering through the aisles, Amber finally found some tanning lotion, which she wasn't all that keen on, cotton balls, and clear nail polish.

Once back in the car, Amber drove into the tourist section of Ensenada, passing Hussong's, where you could hear the loud yells from the drunks in the famous cantina. I didn't want any part of a bar, and I guess they didn't either, for they didn't say anything as we got back on the highway heading north, toward my aunt's trailer.

"On a strong swell and a high tide Pescados breaks good," I said. "Let's hit it on the way back to San Rafael." My theory was that the people staying at my aunt's trailer would be gone by the time we returned. At least that was what I hoped. And there was no reason why we couldn't keep surfing

"Excellent! The coastline curves right before it, so it's protected from the wind," Jamie said.

Pescados was named for the fish cannery at Punta Morro, just north of Ensenada and south of Puntas. As you drive the highway there's a church on the left, before the cannery, in the village. The cannery employs most of the inhabitants, and when the shift changes, the settlement's streets on both sides of the town come alive. A few yards beyond the church is some sort of veterans' hall or something, a big rectangular building that always seems to have music blaring out of its dark innards, and drunks sometimes piss behind the building, which you can see from the water. Just beyond this building, and before the houses, is an alley.

Remembering a joke my uncle told one time when he, Nestor, and I passed the cannery after having gone out on a half-day fishing boat, I said, "Hey, what did the blind man say when he passed the fish market?"

"I give up, what?" Jamie said.

"Hello, girls."

"You're not funny, Juan. In fact you're an ass," Amber said.

Jamie laughed his high hiccup laugh, and I knew that dog had fooled around with that woman.

Before I had a chance to call him on it, Amber turned off the highway into the alley where I'd told her to go, immediately bottoming out the car's undercarriage on the exceedingly rutted roadway. Potholes is an understatement. She inched forward in the shadowed alleyway, almost in the front doors of houses. Most residents didn't have cars, it was obvious, since there were no cars parked back here. Once at the end of the alley, we veered to the right, and we could actually see the waves breaking.

Regular, solid lines moved onto the reef. Pescados is a right-breaking wave, the left simply a walled explosion terminating at the cannery's short pier. Deeper water to the right of the wave lets it hold up longer, thus the right. The sun was low in the sky, and a diamond brightness glinted off the ocean, making the waves invisible at a certain angle. The wind had dropped dramatically, and the small bay was somewhat sheltered, the conditions in the water near perfect. The waves were big and thick and slow, since it was high tide. The only unfavorable aspect about Pescados is that the cannery throws all the unusable fish remains into the water, and there are times when the sea is dappled with sharks. This afternoon was not one of those times — there were no fins visible. I said nothing of this to Amber.

She parked the car, careful not to block entirely the view of the man who sat in the house's doorway, drinking from a quart bottle of beer. Upon leaving the car, we were hit with a barrage of "ocean." Salt-smell infused the air. Gulls landed on large, wet rocks, and then took off again. The sound of the sea hitting the reef and then collapsing forward onto the breakwater-like rocks that protected the houses on this little mesa was overpowering. A noisy constant rush of air and energy, the net result of charged water particles permeating the landscape. And the sweet smell of rotting garbage here and there from the sun-cooked entrails of fish littering the pier just to the north.

I opened the back of the 4Runner to get out our boards. Jamie took his first and walked over the rocks on his way to the sea. Then Amber took hers. As I pulled my board out, I noticed the guy in the doorway attempt to stand. He sat back down. On his next try he remained standing, and then he weaved his way to us.

"Why do you come here?" he asked in Spanish.

"For the waves," I answered.

"This is my home. You come and drink and make fun of us. You smoke the marijuana. You will be arrested if you cause trouble."

"My friends and I do none of these things," I said.

The man tried to focus on Amber, and had trouble. He probably hadn't seen a girl surfer here.

"All of you Americans are the same," he said, but with less conviction.

"We mean no disrespect."

"You have to pay to park here."

"Fine."

"Ten dollars."

"That is a lot of money."

"The ocean is good here, true?"

"Yes, it is very good. I will pay to park here. And we will do none of the things that you mention."

"What is he saying?" Amber said.

"If we park in front of his house, he wants money. He's messed up."

"Let's move the car," Amber said.

"I don't think it's a good idea. Besides, he'll watch it."

Jamie was over the rocks, in the water. After paying the *borracho*, Amber and I made our way into the ocean.

⚬

By the time we came in from surfing, a mist-filtered dusk had overtaken the entire landscape. The alley in which we'd driven to the oceanfront was obscured, shadow forms moving about. In some of the houses a stark white lightbulb hanging from a ceiling lighted the room, while other houses remained dark inside, ethereal shapes moving to and fro. Far off you could hear faint radio music. From the opposite direction you could hear the canned laughter of a television show. Evening in a working-class neighborhood. Gulls squawked, heading to wherever it is they go at dusk. A dog barked. The surf crashed on the rocks below us.

For some reason the thought of home overtook me. A melancholy sense that when I returned it wouldn't be the same. And it wouldn't. My brother was married, moved out. I had taken my family's car. Jamie had fought with and beat up F. Amber had run away with us, and was hanging with me instead of being faithful to Robert Bonham. Who knew what would happen to me for taking the car? I guess it was the darkness approaching, the families gathering to eat their dinners that made me sad. I knew my mother would be making dinner for Nestor and my brother and sister; I hoped they weren't too worried about me. I began feeling guilty for not leaving a real message on the phone machine. Maybe I should buy a phone card or something, try to call again. They had heard my voice, though.

After drying off I put on my sweatshirt. Amber wore her new Indian cotton pullover as she dried her hair with a towel. Jamie peered out at the building waves, still in his wetsuit.

The man who'd extorted our money to park sat in his doorway eating. After he finished his plate he stood up, this time with ease, and made his way to me. His hair was wet and he had clean clothes on. He smelled of aftershave.

"Your money," he said, offering the ten dollars I had given him.

"No, it is fine, I said.

"I insist," the man said. "I am not right these days."

"If you want to charge, that is fine."

"You make no trouble. Others are not so welcome. They have been like pigs when here. We live here, and those who visit should respect our houses," the man said. He still held out the two five dollar bills.

"I agree."

"Take your money."

I remembered attending S.C. football games at the Coliseum in Los Angeles. Nestor would park our car right on the lawn of some family that was making extra money by letting people cover their property with cars. My father paid twenty-five dollars and sometimes more for the luxury of parking very close to the stadium. We were right on top of the waves.

"I will pay five dollars to park. That is fair."

"Fine," the man said. He pocketed one five, giving the other one to me.

"You like the big waves?" he said. His voice, for some reason, reminded me of my grandfather's.

"Oh, yes!" I said.

"I know a very good place," he said.

"Where?" I said.

"In the ocean," he said.

"I see," I said, even though I didn't.

"An island," he said.

"What's he saying?" Jamie grunted from his perch on the rocks.

I could barely see him, what with the blackening sky and the swirling thick mist covering everything. The sea was now slick-black, oily almost, and the waves hitting the rocks exploded with a white, rhythmic frequency, the tide all the way in.

"He says he knows an island where the waves are really good."

"Excellent!" Jamie said.

"That's nice," Amber said, "but last time I checked we didn't have a boat."

Good, Amber, I thought.

"You wish to go?" the man said.

"Yes," I said. "But we have no way of getting there."

"I am a fisherman," the man said. "But recently I have not been fishing. I have been only drinking." He paused and looked out over the now black sea. "I have a dory and will take you tomorrow, if you wish."

"What's he saying?" Jamie asked.

"He says he has a boat and will take us tomorrow."

"Excellent," Jamie said. "Hell, yes!"

I looked at Amber. She shivered. The man's confession worked like a truth serum for me. I wanted to confess to him as well. I've stolen my mother's car! We're on the run! Jamie beat up his step-father! I love Amber!

I said, "What is your name?"

"Jésus," the man said.

CHAPTER 8

We sat before a small fire, right on the point overlooking Puntas, banda music blaring on the only radio station we could get. The fire burned bright and flamed out, and then one of us would feed it some brush and driftwood until the process would repeat itself. It was a dark clear night, and out of the fire's light all you could see was black, except for the sky, which was filled with cosmic treats: the Big Dipper, the Little Dipper, Mars low on the horizon, and billions of other stars and planets and galaxies, even, whose names I didn't know and whose light was reaching this point on Earth after traveling for a longer time than the Earth had even existed, for all I knew.

Jamie had a pint of sloe gin. I hated the shit; it tasted like medicine. We sat on top of sleeping bags, sophisticated drinkers, but, still, sand covered our existence, and that was okay by me.

Amber stretched on a blanket in various yoga poses as Jamie and I watched. Right now she was in a cross-legged forward fold, her head slightly above the sand.

"That's cheap about my aunt's trailer," I said. "Maybe they'll be gone tomorrow. Maybe whoever it is just took a long weekend." I didn't know what the deal was, but those people were still there when we drove back to San Rafael. I might have had a chance had they not been there. I might have been able to set up Jamie at the trailer and then return home with Amber.

"I wonder where that old Mexican will take us?" Jamie said, changing the subject. He didn't seem concerned about what he would do, now that he was down here. All he wanted to do was surf, and he was doing it. I didn't want to leave until he was settled, I knew that much.

"You're so lame. He's not taking *us* anywhere," Amber said, releasing out of her pose at one-eighth speed.

"He's got a boat."

"So he says."

"He probably does," I said.

"See." Jamie sneered at Amber.

"I'm not going out with that drunk," Amber said.

"No problem," I said.

"He won't be drunk tomorrow." Jamie took a big swig of sloe gin. Amber looked at me. Jamie looked up in the sky.

I threw some small pieces of brush on the fire. It sputtered awake. "Jésus."

"Jesus, shit," Jamie said.

"What?"

"His name is Jésus."

"Absolutely. Jesus." Amber lay back on a sleeping bag. She arched her back so that only her shoulders and feet made contact. I could hear her slow, deep breaths.

I sat with my legs crossed, sifting the sandy dirt between my feet.

Jamie stood up a little wobbly and threw a rock over the cliff. You couldn't see it hit water; it was that dark, though you could see the whitewater of breaking waves out in the lineup.

I stretched out my leg, stopping it on Amber's sleeping bag. I stretched farther, until I touched her foot. She came out of her pose and sat up smiling, rubbing my shin, back and forth.

"I don't want to go out on the ocean with that guy," she said.

Jamie took another drink of the gin. "I do."

"Really, Jamie," Amber said. "I don't want to go out on a boat."

"Don't come, then. Juan'll go. Right?"

Amber stood up and walked to the edge of the cliff. She looked over.

I lay down on the sleeping bag, right where she had been seconds earlier.

"Right?" Jamie said much louder.

"I don't know. I've got my mom's car here."

"One more day won't mean shit. It's not like you're *not* in trouble. Whatever happens, happens."

"Stop it, Jamie," Amber said.

I fell for the taunt. "Let's see what his boat is like. One more day won't make that much difference." I hoped the people at my aunt's place would be gone by then; I hoped my parents were . . .

Approaching the fire, Amber said, "Jamie, you think you're Kurtz going farther and farther up the river. Well, you're not! We need to decide some things. Now! How are you going to stay down here? What if that trailer's not . . ."

"What river?" he interrupted her. "We're surfers! And I'll stay right here, surfing."

"Get real."

"I am. Realer than I've ever been in my life." He took another swig from the bottle.

"Don't be so lame!" Amber sat down again on the sleeping bag, right next to me.

Jamie got up, sort of half-walked and stumbled over to my mother's car, rooted around on the floor, came back, and plopped down on his sleeping bag. He pulled something out of his pants pocket. With unsteady fingers he placed it onto a burning branch.

"Where'd you get that?" I could see Amber's bare legs, see the tiny hearts on the gold ankle bracelet she always wore, a gift from Robert Bonham.

Jamie took a hit off the joint and passed it to me.

I hated pot; it makes you stupid and lazy, and that was how I felt now, though I still refused it. I passed it on to Amber but she refused so I passed it back to Jamie.

"Cindy," he said, exhaling smoke.

"Did you get her phone number?" Amber put some more brush on the fire.

Sometimes they would do that, just start talking about a subject that nobody else knew, except for them. One of them would say something, a complete non sequitur, but the other one would be right on track.

Amber placed the paper bag of stuff from the store in front of her, sitting down. She reached under her Indian jacket and unhooked her bra, pulling it out and looking at the back strap. She frowned at it, and then squinted. She opened the nail polish and painted some on the metal hook.

"No. What are you doing?"

"Address?"

"No. What for?"

"Talk to her, write to her."

"Why would I want to do that?"

"What are you doing?" I pretended to be calm in spite of the appearance of her silky black bra.

"This thing's rubbing my back."

"My sunglasses are rubbing my ear," Jamie said.

"Let me see them."

He took off his glasses and tossed them to her. She squinted at them and then painted some nail polish on the curved part.

"Why are things so fucked up?" I said.

Amber looked up in the sky and chuckled.

"My brother got married just because Bonnie's pregnant. Why'd they have to get married?"

"She's pregnant? I didn't know that!" Amber shouted.

"Why'd Mom marry F? *Marry!*"

"Why did you mark up his underwear?" Amber said.

"They were skid marks," Jamie said.

"Shit," Amber said.

"My point exactly."

"It wasn't a very good welcome for him."

"He wasn't welcome."

"He did his flamethrower shit," I said.

"What?" Amber said.

"You know how he always farts? Well, one time when Juan and I had just gotten back from surfing, he spread his legs wide apart, put his butt in the air, and lit his fart with a match. Can you believe it?" Jamie looked to me for commiseration.

"It was foul shit," I said.

"You guys," Amber said.

"Full dick stuff," Jamie said. "Skunk city."

When F had first moved in to Jamie's house after he married Claire, Jamie and I put shoe polish on his underwear. You had to respond, I mean the guy's sitting right where Mr. Watkins used to sit, lighting his farts on fire. My older brother shoe-polished my uncle's underwear when we were younger. My uncle was a farter too. When Jamie and I did it to F's — the asshole wore huge white briefs! — we couldn't stop giggling, and now, when I thought of it again, I giggled.

"It's not funny, Juan," Amber said. "You guys didn't give him a chance. He was trying to help."

"He was gravy training," I said.

"Oh, and you were so good to him, Amber," Jamie said. "You took his coins too."

F went berserk on that one. He had a coin collection, or so he claimed, in a huge glass jar. Jamie and I took coins from the so-called collection any time we wanted money. When the level became noticeably low, F hid the remaining loot somewhere where we couldn't find it. And gave Jamie a tongue lashing. Evidently everyone was raiding those coins.

"He is a jerk," Amber said. "Let me have a beer, then."

We had a cheap foam cooler filled with ice and sodas and a few beers. I opened three bottles and passed them around. Amber took

94

some of Jamie's pot as she handed his glasses back to him. He put them on and leaned back.

We sat there, watching the Baja sky, listening to the sounds of the empty night: waves breaking over the rocks, wind rustling sand and fire, and every so often tires echoing off the pavement up on the road.

Amber did have a point about F. He hadn't always been so bad. In fact, at first, I sort of liked him. He established an account for Jamie at this place that made hamburgers — Bimbo Burgers they were called — miniature hamburgers that were outrageous. Jamie could eat eight at a time, no sweat. I could eat four or five when I was hungry. Any time we wanted, and especially on our way back from surfing, we could stuff ourselves with those little hamburgers. That had been cool on F's part.

There were other things as well. One time F took Jamie, Greg Scott, and me to this all-you-can-eat smorgasbord. It was after surfing, and F insisted on taking us. He paid, and then had to go run some errands. Jamie and Greg and I got down to business, going for the roast beef first, with mashed potatoes. We each had two plates of that, and then went back for turkey plates. By that time I was stuffed, but I just had to get some desert, German chocolate cake. But Jamie wasn't finished. He went back for ham, and then had two salads, and three deserts. When F came back from whatever he was doing, the manager of the place was at our table telling Jamie that he couldn't come back. Greg and I couldn't help cracking up.

Jamie looked sort of embarrassed, when F intervened and said, "What are you talking about? Isn't this all you can eat?"

The proprietor said, yes, it was, but there were limits, and Jamie had exceeded them.

"What limits?" F said.

"Look, I don't want no trouble, okay, but this boy isn't welcome here again."

"Your food tastes like shit anyway," F said. "C'mon, guys."

He followed us out of the big room that was the restaurant, but stopped right in the entryway that separated the eating part from the lobby. And there, before the manager, the staff, and the patrons, he lifted his leg and shook it as if there were something stuck high up in his pants, all the while cutting a huge fart.

We were in the eighth grade and thought that was the funniest thing that would ever happen in our lives. Greg Scott fell on the ground he was laughing so hard. My stomach hurt the next day, I'd laughed so much. But when I told my older brother, he didn't think it was that funny. He said it might have been funny if I had done it, or Jamie or Greg, but he said it wasn't funny when a grown man acted like a kid. Something's off, he'd said.

It was later that I understood what my brother meant. It was like F had missed the day when they taught you boundaries or something. He seemed to understand how to act around adults, but around kids he tried to be one of us, and he wasn't, no way. So it was inevitable that things would go wrong when this dipshit who sometimes outdid the kids tried to assume authority, tried to impart discipline and shit, cause it just didn't wash. And that was Jamie's whole issue. How can you accept advice or punishment from someone when you don't respect them?

Jamie finished his bottle of sloe gin. He lit another joint.

"How much of that shit you got?" I said.

"This is it."

"Do you like her?" Amber wiped her leg where she'd spilled beer. There they went again.

"No. I don't know. I don't even know her."

"I think you do." Amber took another swig of beer.

Jamie lay down. And fell asleep.

"Wake up, asshole," Amber said to him. Then to me she said, "So this is one of your famous surf trips?" Without waiting for an answer she said, "It's a big bore."

"What do you want, nightlife?"

"What do you expect from fif . . ." She caught herself and stopped. She tried to smile at me but I turned away.

She was thinking of Robert Bonham, I bet. Robert Bonham. When he first started taking Amber surfing. He was patient with her, helping her in the way that those who have gone before can help those who are beginning. And he wanted Jamie along to help as well. Robert Bonham figured, Jamie told me, that with the two of them, they could help Amber to get waves, even though she was a beginner. The problem was, however, I wasn't invited. Jamie went with Robert Bonham and Amber once without me, the first time. The second time Robert invited Jamie to go with him and Amber, Jamie declined. He said if I couldn't go, then he wouldn't go either. I remember because I was doing yard work or something, Nestor leading the charge, and I saw Jamie coming over the dirt path in the field next to our house.

I turned off the lawn mower when he got close to me. "I thought you were surfing," I'd said in a snotty voice.

"I didn't go with that cheapskate. Need some help?"

Jamie worked with Nestor and me, helping with the lawn and trimming some bushes and stuff.

When we finished, we rode our bikes back to his house, where we shot some hoops. During an intense game of Horse, Amber showed up with Robert Bonham.

He handed her her board without coming up the driveway.

"Cheapskate," Jamie muttered. And that day, I knew the kind of friend Jamie was. He'd rather not go surfing than leave me behind.

"Not anymore," Amber had said. "You can surf with us from now on, Juan." She had smiled at me.

Remembering that smile from Amber, I had a huge excitement in my gut. My hands were shaking, so I placed them under my bottom. My mouth was dry in spite of the cold beer.

"Look, Juan, I'm sorry, okay?"

I tried to play it cool, and didn't answer.

She stood up and helped her groggy brother get in a sleeping bag. I felt a warmness inside, watching her take care of Jamie. My friend was okay; F couldn't touch him, get him arrested. She helped him into one of the bags — there were only two of them.

When she was finished she came over and sat next to me on the other one.

I looked long and hard into her eyes. Blue. Ice and sky. People would look at Amber and not know if her eyes were green or gray or blue. Different people would give all those colors as their answers, if they were asked. I never really thought about it that much because I knew: they were blue. Why would she want to be with a fifteen-year-old?

"Listen, Amber, let's go check out that island, okay? If those people are still at my aunt's when we come back, I'm leaving. But if they're gone, you and Jamie can stay if you want. But I would like to check out those waves on that island." Why not? When would I ever get another chance like this? If the universe sends you something, take advantage of it, is what I say. Yet the universe hadn't sent me anything: I'd taken it, no doubt about it. I'd taken my mother's car, taken all the money from her purse, used Jamie's misfortune as an opportunity to find a perfect wave.

"Look at Jamie. He thinks we're on vacation or something. We're not, Juan, we're not."

"I know. But the swell's pumping and we're down here. And a guy with a boat? C'mon, when will we ever get a chance like this again? Never. Besides, we could get the perfect wave."

She shook her head. "There's no such thing."

"I think there may be. Why did this fisherman show up? He's gonna take us to an island where the waves are perfect. I can feel it. There's gotta be a perfect wave. Jamie thinks there is."

After a time she said, "Okay, I guess."

We both looked up at the stars, the night filled with them. The wind blew in fresh ocean air over everything. As I inhaled the salt smell I looked down at the one remaining sleeping bag. So did Amber.

"You can sleep with me, Juan, but no fooling around, okay?"

"What about Robert?"

"I don't know," she said.

"I'll try."

"No trying. If you don't agree, then you can sleep over there."

The fire was fading. I got up and fed it all the stuff we'd collected, building a huge, flaming globe. It highlighted Jamie as he drooled on his sleeping bag. It lighted Amber's soft smooth legs, her creamy face. While I fed the fire she laid out the sleeping bag, first shaking the sand out of it.

After I turned off the music we lay side by side on a blanket with a sleeping bag over us, staring into heaven. It was like going to the planetarium at Griffith Park, only much, much better. So vast and ethereal, like a fully formed idea that you can't verbalize. And so quiet.

As the fire burned out, the sky became brighter, until it was so luminous that it had come alive, a swirling, moving mass of entities. Life. Alive. Jamie's, Amber's, and my problems were so inconsequential in the big scheme of things, as the cliché goes. For once I understood it. I was experiencing the "real" right before my very eyes. The night sky, the stars, Amber, Jamie. The now. The moment.

It had a liberating effect.

My family would be okay. I would survive the lapse in good judgment. My mom and dad would get over it. My brother would become a father, I would become an uncle. Jamie would return. Amber . . .

I leaned over and kissed her on the lips. She kissed back, nestling into the crook of my arm, as we began messing around.

CHAPTER 9

The day was melancholy, the sky silently weeping over the vast and unseen ocean. It wasn't what you would call raining, and it wasn't really foggy, but the fact remained that everything was all wet, and a light, filtering mist dusted the ocean. Huge smooth-thick swells would hump up, and then we'd freeboard down their backsides.

Jésus worked the helm, which was in the center toward the stern of the dory. The bow and stern had points to them, mostly keeping out the seas that we bobbed forward on. A Mercury outboard engine made the dory very fast indeed when he gunned it, and there were three sides and a roof to the tiny wheelhouse in which Jésus stood, intent and braced against the swell. A thick tarp stretched from the bow to the wheelhouse, and Amber slept under its sheltering dryness. Jamie sat on the bait tank in the stern, looking back at the direction from which we'd come. I stood in between Jésus and Jamie.

As we had motored out of the harbor Jamie had said to me, "I know what's going on with you and my sister."

"What? What's going on?"

"Don't play stupid, Juan. I know what's up, so knock it off."

"I'm not good enough for your sister? Is that it? Is that what you're saying? Listen, a-hole, she's old enough to make her own decisions and so am I. *Comprenez-vous, cabrone?*"

"What about Robert?"

"Fuck Robert."

"Just fuck off, Juan."

He had made for the bait tank, and I had remained next to the wheelhouse by Jésus.

We'd not spoken for quite some time. None of the Watkins were talkative, and I don't know why. When he was alive Mr. Watkins would exclaim a lot after he'd drunk a few martinis, his drink of choice. Mrs. Watkins was quiet most of the time I saw the family interacting when I'd eat dinner with them. In fact, their meal routine was wholly different from that of my family. In my family we'd practically fight over the food when it was put on the table. My little brother and sister would get yelled at, most likely sent to their rooms for screwing up the sanctity of the meal. Everyone in my family would talk at once, making the most dominant one raise their voice. In my family people would shout their conversations from different sides of the house! But in general, mealtime was abuzz with laughter and talk. Not so at Jamie's. Everyone was tight-lipped.

Jamie had a double reason for not being talkative. Besides the quiet family thing, he had had a lisp when he was young. He used to get taken out of class to attend a speech class. The therapist told him he had a lazy T, and that he'd most likely outgrow it, which he did. It was most pronounced in kindergarten, though it improved steadily as he got older. I never had any trouble understanding him, but some of our teachers did. So he learned to keep quiet rather than call attention to his lisp. The lisp and his shy nature didn't make for a very outgoing person when we were younger. But he still preferred not to talk, if given a choice.

Amber was different. She was so smart that most shit wasn't worth her bother. Whereas Jamie's silence was genetic and physical, Amber's was genetic and social. Most people were too stupid to talk to, she'd once said. A lot of kids thought she was weird. She went from cheering squad to yoga. She surfed, though a lot of girls did that, but she could rip. And she was really good-looking. All these things created a sort of unapproachable air, an aloofness that turned off people. So they said mean things about her, said she was stuck-up, said she had a stick up her butt, said she was snotty, said she thought she was better than everyone else (she did), all the stuff jealous people say when they don't know someone and don't know how to relate to them.

None of it bothered Amber, and that made things worse, somehow. It's like if you don't care, that makes the dolts even angrier. What did Amber care? She and Robert Bonham were inseparable.

And she had Jamie.

Now she had me. Which Jamie was against.

Jamie was doing some weird shit, though I knew he wouldn't turn on me. I'd never even had such a thought before, but he'd changed so much lately. It wasn't that I was afraid of him; I wasn't. I was terrified. Jamie was a really good fighter.

Last year, when Jamie and I were in the ninth grade, this guy who was a junior, Kent Chambers, got in a fight with Jamie. Jamie hadn't wanted to fight, hadn't done anything to start it or encourage it. In fact, he'd done everything short of running away to get out of it. It happened like this: Jamie and Greg Scott and I and some other guys were hanging by the eucalyptus trees, away from everyone else, just being freshman, just trying not to cause attention, when the shit broke out. We didn't even see what happened, but this twerp, Brad Patton, ran by us, charging into the crowd over by the Coke machines. Next thing we knew Kent Chambers and some of his bros are right in our faces.

"Who threw it?" Kent Chambers was pissed. His face was all red and he had food on his shirt.

None of us said anything. We all just sort of looked at the ground, looked off in the distance, anywhere but at the crowd of juniors that now surrounded us.

"Which one of you fuckheads threw it! Who's eating burritos?" He looked right at me.

Still no answer. Except Jamie had just finished one, and the wrapper lay at his feet. I tried to sidle over and cover it with my tennis shoe, but it was too late — Kent Chambers had seen it as well.

"Okay," Kent Chambers said, "the tall one," meaning Jamie, because he'd had his growth spurt before any of us.

Jamie finally looked up, looked Kent Chambers in the eye. "I didn't throw anything."

Kent Chambers wasn't a gangster or anything, wasn't a tough guy. I think he was an okay guy. But he was older, and I sure didn't want to fight him. He was just bigger than we were, just stronger.

"One of you assholes did, and it was you."

And just like that, he came at Jamie. Hard and fast. Throwing down.

Jamie backed around the tree, saying, "I don't want to fight."

Kent kept coming, and other kids sensed something going on and began charging over.

Kent pushed Jamie away from the tree, where he had no cover. Some of the eleventh-grade guys thought it was cool, some of them wanted to join in, and one guy shook his head and left. A school yard's no different from a barnyard, so I've heard, and the violent excitement brought kids streaming toward us.

"I don't want to fight," Jamie said again.

"You threw a burrito, you dick!" Kent said coming at Jamie for real.

Jamie stood his ground, put his hands up, and sidestepped Kent's first sortie, hitting Kent in the jaw with a really good blow.

Kent was briefly spun around, but he turned to face Jamie, this time even more enraged, if that were possible. They went at each other again, this time Jamie coming forward, both of them with their fists going off.

Next thing I knew Kent Chambers was on the ground, Jamie was over him, and the campus police officer had a hold of Jamie by the shoulder. Kent's face had big welts on it. Jamie's T-shirt was ripped and he looked zoned out, looked as if he didn't know what had had happened. Jamie was quick, though. And I knew he had had a lot of anger always stored inside because of his father, and then because of F.

Before the end of lunch bell rang, Amber came rushing up to me. We were still under the eucalyptus tree where it had all started.

Usually Amber wouldn't talk to Jamie and me at school. She wouldn't ignore us or anything, she just didn't go out of her way to associate with us.

"Is he okay?" she said, breathless. "I heard he fought Kent Chambers."

I felt really cool, a junior girl seeking me out and everything. And Jamie had kicked Kent Chambers's ass! "Yeah, he's fine. Somebody threw something on that guy and he insisted Jamie had done it."

"He's okay, Juan? He's not hurt?"

"Naw, he won!" I couldn't help chuckling, though I stopped it when I looked over at Kent Chambers's boys, who didn't look too happy with us.

"Okay," Amber said.

Jamie was sent home, and suspended for two days, but I went over to his house right after school to see him. He was sort of depressed about getting suspended, and felt weird about kicking some guy's ass for nothing. Claire hadn't wanted to let me in at first. Not because of me. It was because she didn't want to reward him for fighting. When I told her the story, she relented.

When F returned home from work, he called Jamie into the TV room, where Jamie told him what happened. Things were already pretty strained between Jamie and F because Jamie resented F's attempts at fathering him. This time was different, however.

"What'd he say?" I asked Jamie when he returned to his room.

"He said I had a right to defend myself."

"Are you in more trouble?"

"No."

"Cool."

We hung out some more, playing video games and listening to music. When it was almost dinnertime I took off for home. The really strange thing was, before I got off Jamie's street, I saw Kent Chambers pass me in his car, which stopped at Jamie's. I saw Kent Chambers knock on the door, and someone answer the door, and then the door close again. Then the door opened and I saw F talking on the porch with Kent Chambers. When F went back in the house and Kent Chambers didn't leave, I walked back closer to Jamie's house.

It was dusk, but you could still see things pretty well. And what I saw shocked me. F and Jamie were now on the front porch. I was too far away to hear what they said, but Jamie told me later when I called him. Kent Chambers thought it was just luck, the reason Jamie had won their fight in school. He wanted to fight Jamie again, to see if this were true.

Jamie didn't want to fight, I could see that much. But then Kent Chambers moved off the porch and F shoved Jamie out onto the front lawn with Kent Chambers, where they fought again, and once again Jamie kicked his ass. Even better this time, for Jamie was mad, he later told me, mad at F for forcing him to fight, mad at Kent Chambers for showing up at his house. F said it would make him a man. What kind of a stupid adult makes you fight? Mr. Watkins would have sent Kent Chambers on his way. But F was in that house and Jamie had had to fight. More sick shit à la F.

❧

I didn't want to intrude on Jamie's brooding, and, besides, he was just crabby from the pot and his hangover, I reasoned, because he couldn't get mad at me. I certainly didn't want to bother Jésus as he navigated us toward La Isla de los Delfíns, our destination.

It had been late morning by the time we'd left Ensenada Harbor, heading straight into the fog bank that hovered just offshore. Amber had made for the bow, where she got under the tarp and immediately went to sleep. As I watched her now her bare toes twitched from underneath a sleeping bag as she slept on. Her feet, even in repose, were pigeon-toed.

On and on the outboard droned, up and down, up and down we moved in the heightened, electrically charged seas. The great expanse of ocean made me think about my family. And my decision-making process. Were they worried about me? Were they surprised at my behavior? Shit, had I done the right thing? What were Jamie's thoughts as he sat with his head down and his shoulders bowed, contemplating what? And Jésus. What did he think? He'd told me that he lost his wife and child, that he no longer felt the urge to live, that he did not feel the need to fish. They had died in a bus accident. "It will be good for me to get away from my memories," he had told me.

With a bunch of rustling, Amber awoke, making her way back to the stern. "Where the hell are we going? Ugh, I don't feel well."

I was slightly queasy from the rolling seas even though I'd been on numerous fishing expeditions with my father.

"Hi, Sheila," Jamie said.

"We're almost there," I said.

"Where is 'there'?"

"The island with the perfect wave," Jamie said.

"He never said that," I said. "Jésus said the waves were good."

"What, exactly, did Mr. Jesus say?"

I looked Amber in the eye. "He said the waves were very good."

"Translate what he said exactly," she said. Her hair was flattened on one side, and she had small bags under her eyes.

"I can't. He said the waves were big, and the fishermen call the place 'clouds' or something like that. It's on the island we're going to."

Jamie said, "Excellent."

Amber shook her head. "Instead of the great white whale, you guys are in search of the great wave."

"Good, Amber."

"We're in search of a perfect wave," Jamie said.

And we were, I supposed. I figured that was what kept me going farther and farther south, getting in bigger and bigger trouble. The night the shit went down with F, I knew that a swell was building. I knew about the hurricane off Hawai'i. I knew that it would hit the West Coast in a few days. I knew the swell would be perfect about now, and I also knew the waves would be best down south, and certainly less crowded.

But what is a perfect wave? The perfect wave? Is my perfect wave the same perfect wave for Jamie? Or does it change from person to person? And say you did surf *the* perfect wave — what would be left to live for?

❦

The droning engine mesmerized us into some sort of complacency. We sat in our places, pondering our individual situations, I guessed. Jésus was dry in the tiny wheelhouse, calm and stoic, given *his* situation. My hair was wet, and so was Jamie's. Amber had gone back under the tarp, and I could see her feet working back and forth, back and forth, as if she were walking on land in all her pigeon-toed glory.

At some point the drizzle stopped, and the fog became less thick, and it appeared as if we might ride out of the clouds, but we didn't. As the fog became denser and rain began to fall, we were suddenly out of the cloud and right before a small island. Everything was in Technicolor: the water and sky a heartbreaking blue, a vibrant blue, and the arid island was alive with magical cacti and succulents. The land was brown and rocky and the coves we could see from the water were calm.

Jamie looked at me.

I smiled at him.

No waves, he mouthed.

I shrugged.

Jésus said that we would make camp in the cove we now approached. Quite narrow and small — I thought of the fjords in Scandinavia — our landing cove didn't seem too inviting; it seemed that there were a bunch of such coves, small fingers of land jutting right into the sea. There was no surf.

"Where are the dolphins?" I said.

"In another cove," Jésus said.

Amber must have felt the engine throttling down, for she emerged from underneath the tarp, rubbing her face, wearing her cutoff Levi's and the Baja jacket. She looked at me and then up into the cove.

"He says the dolphins are in another cove."

"There's no surf on this island," Jamie said.

Silence followed Jésus cutting the engine as we lunged forward when the dory beached itself. Then: a seabird squawking, ocean ripples lapping the boat's sides, hard sun warming you. Brown world to the front, blue world above and behind.

After tilting the outboard up on the transom, he jumped in the shallow water. I followed him, though when my feet hit sand my legs still felt as if they were moving. Amber jumped out, followed by Jamie, all of us helping Jésus pull the dory farther up onto the beach. And then we began unloading. Sleeping bags, cooler, blankets, surfboards, and shopping bags, all the stuff that would sustain us, all settled on the sand far up from the high tide line in the dinky cove. The hillside seemed inordinately steep from this vantage point, and the succulents that lined the cove were oozing a clear liquid from their bright blooms.

We all exerted ourselves, moving our things up the beach toward the dirt cliff, which had a flat sandy plateau on top. Jésus said that weather conditions and swell conditions changed very rapidly on this island, at this place in the ocean, and that waves could appear in this cove if the swell changed direction. "The waves are in the next cove," he said. "Over those sand dunes is another bay, a place where the dolphins mate. The waves are very big there."

I explained what he'd said to Jamie and Amber.

"Let's rip, dudes," Jamie said.

Amber flipped him off.

We took our boards and began climbing the steep canyon sides. While we climbed we saw Jésus relaunch the dory; he was going to fish for dinner; we would meet back here at dusk.

At the top of the canyon we looked south and saw dunes about a quarter of a mile off. We marched across the mesa, and then through the dunes, Jamie with his T-shirt wrapped over his head like Lawrence of Arabia or something.

"Excellent!" he would shout every so often.

"Why don't you get a new adjective," Amber said.

She was having trouble keeping up, so I'd slacken my pace, which would make Jamie stop entirely, and that was when he would bellow, "Excellent!"

When we finally crossed the mesa, the sight we beheld was truly something: a small bay alight with glittering, skittish diamonds. A peak wave breaking wonderfully both right and left and then walling up into a very fast and steep shorebreak. A slight offshore wind blew the tops of the waves back upon themselves. And this: the entire surface rippled with dolphin life. Cows and calves and bulls roaming over the very large waves that broke with a regularity and clarity that I'd never before seen, certainly never imagined could exist.

"Oh," said Amber.

"Yeah," Jamie said.

I stood by them, my friend and his sister, mute with delight and anticipation. I'd been feeling really guilty about my actions, and hoped that my family wasn't too worried about me. But when I stood on that mesa, my feet resting in the warm sand, watching the dolphins and the breaking waves, I was truly glad I'd done all the things that got us here, made the decisions I'd made. I looked at Jamie and my heart was glad that he was safe. Amber, well, Amber could be my girlfriend!

Dolphins took off on swells, body surfing the drop, dolphin-kicking on the face, riding all the way to the shorebreak, where they'd dive under, reappearing out the backside of the wave.

I began running down the sand dune's face, heading for the beach. Jamie passed me, flying down the gentle hill, and I could hear Amber right behind as we all made for the surf.

Paddling out through the channel and watching the huge waves break was an exercise in controlled anticipation. These were the largest waves any of us had seen, and it was difficult to gauge their actual size until someone rode one of the mackers. Here, away from where they hit shallower reef water, the swells would lift you up, up, giving you a drop of weightlessness as they passed underneath. Even off to the side of the breaking waves in the safe confines of the channel.

In the break the waves were majestic arms of power, swept from God knows where by some out-of-control circular winds. These waves, though much slower than the winds of the hurricane, were extensions of it — for every action there is an equal and opposite reaction. There were many waves in a set, the takeoff was steep but makeable, and these waves, I was sure, were the largest I'd ever ride. I was excited. I was scared. So much for my wish to die before I was eighteen, and to die in waves, which I'd sometimes fantasized about.

Jamie told Amber to ride waves between sets, smaller things that didn't have the raw power of the chunkers that hit the rock reef we neared. She'd agreed, but as I watched her paddle I didn't think she'd stick to it because she moved forward in steady, sure strokes, mesmerized by the grace and splendor of the sea.

On the paddle out we didn't speak for we were too busy sizing up the break. Which cliché would work to describe it? A postcard? That would work, except there are no surfing postcards with this bay on them, that's for sure. The sky was a blue I'd never seen before, a blue that deep-water sailors probably take for granted. Far away toward the mainland, which you couldn't see, huge white clouds amassed as they passed over mountaintops. And the water. You could see the smooth rocks way below, see reef fish darting about, see the high and bending sea grass sway in the balletlike tug and pull of the swell.

The wave hit the reef, jumped up, and then cascaded down upon itself in a tumbling wall of whitewater moving in both directions, right and left, increasing in speed and getting more hollow as the water became shallower in toward shore. Finally the entire wave would close out in a massive shorebreak. So we'd had to time our paddle out to make it over the shorebreak, which was larger than the largest waves I'd ever surfed.

We paddled over and into the lineup at the tail end of a set, but Jamie sprinted into one of the last waves, catching it, and howling as he took the drop, lost from sight for a very long time.

Amber and I watched for his board to pop up, but it didn't, he rode on and on; toward shore we could see his head when he'd climb back up to the top of the wave. After he kicked out I relaxed, though he was so far away he looked too small, like a mountain climber who has left the group to go it solo, and is very far up the mountain.

"Richtering," Amber said, her first comment on entering the lineup.

She was right, and I chuckled rather than shit my pants. "It's makable, slow, until the shorebreak. You can do it."

The back of the wave Jamie had caught was huge, like a round pipe, like something those big trucks on the freeway haul and take up two lanes and go really slow. From behind, our perspective, the wave was at least eight or ten feet. The face must have been at least fifteen feet, maybe larger upon hitting the reef and spewing up and out.

When we'd first entered the water the dolphins had gathered their young, herding them out and away from our approach. Some of the larger ones had stuck around, checking us out, though none of them remained in the lineup.

Amber sat on her board, alternately looking in toward shore and then out to sea. Since we were in the lineup, if we miscued our position in relation to the break we'd get hit full force with the breaking wave's impact. Every set would be slightly different, as would each wave, cascading over itself in a slightly different place, depending upon size, tide fluctuations, wind conditions. It was a tricky business just being in the lineup in large surf, not to mention a place you'd never even heard of the day before, a day that was so far removed from our ordinary consciousness as to be dreamlike all the way.

At our own beachbreak you can duck dive under waves that break in front of you. Just bury your nose, diving underneath the whitewater and thus maintaining your position, as it were, rather than getting pushed in too far by the breaking wave. If the waves are too big, they simply rip your leash right off your ankle or the board, though I'd never been in waves that big. Duck diving under these waves was not an option — you couldn't get deep enough! And they'd tear the leash away in nothing flat. I'd once read that storm waves breaking on the North Shore of Hawai'i, if harnessed, could light a medium-sized city for a day. That was a lot of E, and I wouldn't want to get zapped by it, that was for sure! So stay away from where the impact was, at all costs, even if it meant a very long paddle. And there was another issue. Even if you could make it with your board, you wouldn't be able to breathe. The whitewater would be really high, and even though it wasn't all technically water, you wouldn't be able to breathe in that much turbulence.

"Amber, if you wipe out, just dive for the bottom. It'll be calmer down there. Remember, no matter how long you stay down, your board will float; it'll want to surface; just climb up your leash. Stay in the whitewater and get pushed into shore."

"Thanks, Juan. I'm going to eat it, is that what you're saying?"

A set was coming, wavy lines on the horizon getting closer, and the only thing to do was to ride one. We were surfers, and this was what we did.

"The first wave will be smaller," I said. "You catch it. I'll be right behind you."

Squinting into the sun, trying to get a fix on the approaching waves, she sat with her board buried in the water, her hair glistening, her strong shoulders contrasting with the horizon. I wanted to paddle next to her, put my arms around her, and kiss her before

God and the sun, before Jamie, before everyone, and declare my love for her. I was in love! Maybe it was just this day, or the freedom of leaving everything behind and being in a different country. Yes, that was it, a different country, the country of love, and here came a wave so I didn't do any of the above things.

You jockey for the most expedient position: you need to be close to where the wave will begin to curl over itself as it breaks. If you're too far back from this point, you won't be able to paddle into the wave. Too close to the breaking place and the wave will eat you, or you won't be able to take the drop. Too far out, no wave. Too far in, disaster. And this: what the wave itself is doing not in relation to shore, but in relation to the reef. The way it peels off, right and left. These are your considerations, and all you really have to go by is the paddle out. But Jamie has successfully ridden one already, and he is almost back in the lineup, but he's moved too far over toward the peak, and is not far enough out; and you can't worry about Jamie — he'll take care of himself.

"Do you want to wait, Amber? I'll take off first."

"I'm going for it." She swiveled her too-small board, got it planing on top of the water, and began stroking for shore. The hump she raced caught her, lifted her high, high, and then she was gone.

I watched too long, because I wanted to catch the next wave but wasn't in position. Nor for the next two waves. I caught the fourth wave of the set, and it was larger than the previous ones, I figured, for it seemed forever that I took the drop. But I took it smoothly, and when at the bottom of the wave, I rolled my knees and cranked my whole body right into the enormous wall of green that was my life, and it was then that I felt more so than heard this echoing *clunk!* A huge and old dolphin broke the surface, right beside me, nudging my board. We made eye contact, and I saw his gray muzzle, saw his wise eyes that seemed to know the very secrets of nature, and I was so surprised I hesitated, and my hesitation threw me off, literally, for next thing I knew, I'd hit the water, and it felt like cement. I skipped forward a few beats, and then the whitewater crunched me. In an instant I hit rock. Right on my shoulder.

I was out of breath, and just a little scared, for it's not every day that you ride the biggest wave of your life and wipeout and hit bottom because of a playful dolphin. But there it was, I'd already done the worst thing that could happen, and I was still kicking, as they say. I clawed my way to the surface, meeting turbulent resistance all the way. When I reached air, I hungrily gulped it down, grateful to be among the living and the noisy. My board was gone, the leash ripped right off. You wouldn't think that a resounding energy noise would permeate everything, but it did. It roared, like listening in a conch shell, but the conch shell is the universe, and the sea is angry. The next wave was on me so I dove once again, but this time I headed in to shore at the same time. Each successive wave became easier, and soon I was away from the impact zone, where the energy was, and I was able to enjoy the water and the air, and the foam that enveloped me in toward shore.

After that first wipeout we all relaxed somewhat. Someone had to catch the first wave and make it. Someone had to wipe out and survive. After that the mystique was broken, so to speak, and we knew that our ability would take us through the rough spots. Swimming ability, surfing ability. Now we could relax and have fun, which was what we did, even though the waves seemed huge to us.

And in small increments more and more dolphins returned to the lineup, like inquisitive and shy dogs, checking us out, somewhat leery, but riding waves with us. While we talked in between sets, they would sometimes bump our boards, bump our legs, and when we took off they would shadow us, riding up and down on the face of the wave, breaking the surface, and then going under the sheen of the moving surface, chattering, always chattering.

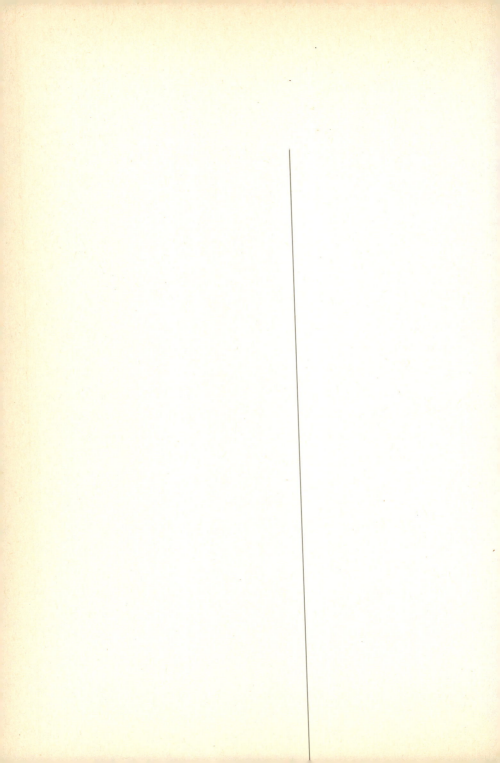

CHAPTER 11

Sometimes when I dream, I dream of dolphins. Being tugged and pulled and played with. Once, I dreamed that a dolphin was giving me artificial respiration. In all the dreams water is the medium. And the dolphins are benign.

It was late afternoon, an early dusk. The reason for the dusklike conditions was because of all the water particles filling the air. It was almost like being at the foot of a gigantic waterfall, with so much water detonating right over the reef. The sun was lower in the sky; the swell had increased with a regular and consistent pattern, so that the last wave Jamie had caught and that I had watched while paddling out was at least three times as big as he was — maybe eighteen feet! The largest wave I'd surfed that day had a twelve-to-thirteen-foot face, over twice my height. Our confidence level was great, and we were riding the waves not just to make them, but with abandon and style. Amber too was caught up in our exhilaration at riding big surf — I'd seen her make some rides that were ten feet at least, though she'd just taken a bad wipeout and was at present tentative.

We'd talked about it on the paddle out. And she agreed that she was now frightened — she had been held under too long — and that it would be best to go in. The day was about over anyway. I beat Jamie back out into the lineup, caught a nice little ten-foot wave, and began the paddle out for one more wave, since I was thoroughly exhausted.

Jésus's name for this break had been something about *Las Nubes,* something I didn't quite catch. The clouds? At the time I made a cloud connection. How a fisherman would know that such good surfing waves existed here I couldn't say. But he did, and we were on cloud nine. No matter how much trouble I'd be in for coming down here, for taking my mother's car, it was worth it. These waves were perfect. I was still having trouble envisioning myself on a fifteen-foot wave that looked like Sunset Beach, Hawai'ian North Shore winter. Had a photographer been with us, Jamie or I might have been on the cover of a surf mag. The last wave Jamie had ridden should have been a "cover" wave. It towered over him, and the face was so large that the top tumbled over itself two or three times until it hit the trough. And Jamie rode it with his casual, stoic style, as if he hadn't a care in the world. As if he were bored, almost.

I thought all these thoughts while paddling out for the last time that day. I did become aware of the fact that the dolphins were no longer around. Probably gone to that communal dolphin sleeping place. And as I paddled out, at peace, Jésus's name for this break hit me like a hard tackle in football. Clouds. The clouds. Jésus had said a Spanish idiom whose meaning I didn't get, something I couldn't understand. I couldn't have understood it. Nobody could have. And I supposed the clouds was the appropriate sentiment regarding this wave. The *real* wave. The wave Jésus meant. For looming way outside, maybe a quarter mile off the beach, was an approaching monstrosity of water. We'd been surfing the inside reef! The small stuff. Now, the second reef was going to break!

And this: Jamie had caught that last huge wave quite a bit farther out than the previous ones.

The wave that now formed walled up the entire bay, threatening to close it out. The swell was so large, from my perspective, that the entire horizon was cut off by the rising wave. The surf had been building all day, I figured, and it would culminate with the "real" reef breaking, the second reef, coincidentally at sunset.

Jamie had deduced all this well before I had, and he was paddling like a madman, heading north and out. Out to sea, out to beat the breaking wave. North toward deeper water, if the bottom held true. I was sort of in the middle. I didn't really want to surf that outside wave, not in the way that Jamie did. (Die in big surf, ha!) But I was too far out in the bay to be safe. And if the wave broke right on me, I didn't think I'd be able to survive its force. I began paddling faster, not wholly committed the way Jamie was, so small and now far away. At that moment I wished that we were together, and that we hadn't disagreed about Amber and me. I looked in toward shore but couldn't see her.

The approaching waves moved so fast and were so large that I had nothing in my experience with which to compare them. Surely I would *not* be far enough out to make it over their crests. Because of his commitment early on, Jamie was okay, and he was now paddling toward the center of the bay, where our takeoff point had been, though it had been much farther in. He was far, far away, in deep water, at the outer reaches of the cove, maybe parallel with the two jutting points that created the bay. I was inside where the new waves would break. Where the impact would be.

It's daunting to find out that the whole day's big-wave surfing was a warm-up, a passing of time, a pause, for the real thing. And Jamie was in position to ride the real thing. Jamie was committed. I was scared, stuck halfway in, halfway out, in never-never land. Not far enough out to make it over the waves, and not far enough in to be safe when they broke. Jamie could paddle right out of the bay, if he chose, and be entirely safe. Amber should be on the beach by now. I was fucked.

Though committed. I was paddling for all I was worth . . . *in*. Chicken of the Sea. But there wasn't a choice, I reasoned later. And there wasn't. The result of my hesitation early on. I was, for sure, a surf coward.

The first wave's whitewater roared over me like an exploding locomotive, ripping my board from me as easily as you lift a newborn. I didn't know which way was up or down; I was in a swirling mass of turbulence, and I couldn't breathe and I couldn't swim.

I'd planned on bailing off my board and diving for the bottom, but since I was paddling in I couldn't see the wave behind me. When there's that much water and it's all moving toward land, and it's just released all its energy — the energy that it stored on its long ocean trip — the forces are very great indeed. The water moving in toward shore must have been traveling at the rate of an automobile, say, getting on the freeway, and I was in the water and had no inkling of such power. No previous experience.

I swallowed ocean water, and coughed, and panicked, and don't remember much from the experience. Except one visual: Jamie taking the drop on the largest wave I could ever imagine. One, two, three, four, five times his body's height. Or maybe I made up the size, I don't know. Thirty, forty feet on the face? I don't know. I was in the water. Disoriented. Adrenaline flooding. On autopilot survival mode. In the clouds, for that amount of water going up and going down and exploding sideways gives you the feeling of being in the air at twenty thousand feet in clouds, weightless, yet unable to breathe.

Jamie freefell, with his feet still on his board, though it wasn't grounded in water. Down and down and down he went until the preternatural barrel covered him on his descent.

CHAPTER 12

"Juan," Amber whispered.

My head rested in her lap. We were on sand. My throat burned. My head ached. She rocked me back and forth. I shivered a full-body shiver. As I came to I moved out of her embrace.

"Where's Jamie?"

"I didn't know if you were coming back," she said. She looked out in the bay.

I looked there too. It was almost dark, and huge white explosions Richtered the sand, vibrating the entire bay. It was closed out, a solid white wall of nuclear foam from point to point. Closed out!

"Where's his board?"

"Jamie's not in yet."

Maybe he'd swum outside to deeper water. I'd heard of guys getting their boards after tremendous wipeouts in big waves, waves in which you didn't wear a leash. Some sort of big-wave phenomenon in which the board sort of gets "stuck" close to the wipeout spot. Maybe that happened. Maybe Jamie was outside.

"Did you see his wave?"

She shook her head. "I can't see out there. Must have been some wave you lost your board on."

"I thought I saw Jamie take off," was all I said.

From shore, and in this light, nobody could get what was happening outside. I couldn't explain to Amber what happened to me, much less what I'd seen her brother do. "He probably paddled out to deeper water. He's not around?"

"No. But I've been with you. A dolphin swam you to shallow water."

"Say what?"

"A dolphin swam you in."

"Don't give me any shit, Amber."

"I'm not." She was serious. Her jaw was set and her eyes hard, and her hair was blowing about her back and face.

"Let's scan the beach." I stood up, feeling sick to my stomach, and I ran away from Amber, retching as I ran, and it felt good to get the saltwater out.

Amber's board was way up on the beach. Mine was getting hit by whitewater, coming in and then going out and crashing on the sand. Amber grabbed it and pulled it close to hers. As she lifted it I could see that the entire nose had broken off, the fiberglass dangling yet still clinging to a chunk of foam like a banana peel holding onto a chunk of banana.

Looking alternately out to sea and up on the dry sand, we walked to the far point; Jamie's board was not visible. So we went to the other point, the direction toward camp. Nothing. And we could no longer see the outside reef break, only hear it, feel that tremendous blast of energy unload in the bay — there was water everywhere, the fog coming back in, the light fading.

A helpless, desolate feeling began to sink in as I felt just how far removed we were from civilization, from things known and loved, things familiar.

The air was warm, but I was cold. I put on my shirt over my wetsuit and looked at Jamie's T-shirt and sunglasses lying on the dark sand. Not so many hours ago he'd had it wrapped around his head; I could still hear him shout "excellent!" if only as an echo.

"Is he outside? Is he beyond the break?" She squinted, trying to see through the fog.

"I bet he is. His board's not on shore. If he's with his board he's okay."

"He's stupid enough to paddle out, isn't he?"

"It wouldn't have been stupidity." It would have been the smartest move he could have made, I thought. How could he have taken off on that wave? How could he paddle back out through those monstrous waves? If anybody could do it, Jamie could. He was a surfer, unlike me. I had acted like a coward. Jamie had confronted the waves, the entire ocean. I had turned tail and ran.

"We should check the cove," Amber said.

"Maybe he paddled there."

We both felt we should remain in the bay of the dolphins, in case Jamie made it to shore. But we knew he could make it back to camp, should he find himself on dry land. Still, I didn't want to leave. "Let's walk the beach one more time."

So we did. It was now thoroughly dark with the thinnest line of purple to the west where the sun had split. As we walked I entertained a fantasy in which Jamie was already back at camp, eating dinner, ready to razz us for our sentimental missteps.

Walking on that dark and deserted beach with Amber I remembered a time when Jamie and I had played Little League. Our team made the playoffs. After our first game, a game we won 5–4, a bunch of the players from the other team showed up on bikes at our park. I had ridden my bike; Jamie had been dropped off by his mother. My bike was surrounded by those boys we had defeated. It seemed as if the park was deserted that Sunday, none of our friends or teammates around.

Jamie and I stayed by the entrance to the gym, watching the boys who came from the next town. They threw us some taunts, and it was obvious what they wanted — blood! We had beaten them, and their season was over. We would play next weekend. So much for sportsmanship, I thought as I looked at my lonely bike. A kid sat on it. At least it was locked, though things weren't looking good.

To make matters worse, Mrs. Watkins pulled up and honked for Jamie. She idled in the street, not ten feet from the thugs.

"I guess I have to go," Jamie said. His forehead was furrowed. "What are you going to do?"

"I don't know," I said.

His mother honked again.

"Why don't you call your mom or dad?"

"They're not home."

"Uh."

This time when Mrs. Watkins honked she kept her hand on the horn. The thugs loved that. "Hey, you big baby, your mama's here!" one of them yelled. Others flipped us off.

Jamie just looked at me and then ran down the steps to the waiting car.

I thought it was all over. I counted the boys around my bike; there were seven, almost a baseball team. As I watched those boys a wonderful thing happened. Not only did Jamie and his mother not drive away, they both got out of the car, Mrs. Watkins opening the trunk. Jamie walked back up the stairs toward me, motioning me to come.

My heart soared as I ran to the bike rack and unlocked my bike. The boys moved back, and didn't say a word as Jamie walked with me. After we put my bike in the trunk, we drove away with the defeated punks yelling and flipping us the bird.

Jamie had come back for me. And I knew I should paddle back out for him. I knew I should go back for him, however futile the gesture might be, but I couldn't make myself enter that angry ocean again. Nothing could get me to act, sort of like my nonresponse when F attacked Jamie on the sand.

Finally, when it was that night-black that must have been the only known vista to pre-twentieth-century people, we climbed out of the bay and onto the mesa. We walked and walked through the black void, unable to find the right cove. The fog bank had come in, hugging the coastline, shrouding each tiny fjord in a cocoon blanket so that we couldn't see the outline of anything, much less our camping gear. But the most frightening aspect was the sound of waves crashing on the coastline, where before there had been no waves.

When we stumbled upon the right cove we found that Jésus was not there. No sign of him or his boat. Waves crashed close to shore, threatening our camp, in spite of the fact that we had pulled everything to the highest point on the beach. So in the dark Amber and I moved everything up onto the mesa.

I gathered some brush and made a small fire. We sat before it, trying to eat, but neither of us had an appetite. We were more dazed than hungry, and we were on an uninhabited island, far out in the sea. Jamie was lost, our ride back to civilization not here. For the first time I felt the loneliness of that poor girl and her brother, the ones left on the island of the blue dolphins. I thought I heard Amber sniffle, and it could have been because of the fog, because it had made its way onto the mesa, obscuring the world in a wet haze, making you feel like crying. The silence and the pathetic fire and the dampness of the night and the loss of the magical night sky all had the effect of making me want to weep. But I wouldn't, not in front of Amber.

At some point we both got under the sleeping bag, happy for human touch, human embrace, and it felt as if we were the only two people on Earth, as if no one could ever find us, and that we would never find our way home.

And then we had sex. No preliminaries, no messing around, just fast fierce love, my first time. It was quick and it was so sweet and wet, and when it was over the nightmare reality of our situation set in once again.

Simply because we could, we did it again later. Had things been different . . . But then I thought of Jamie's disapproval that Amber and I were together. He wasn't here; we were together. Jamie wasn't around.

It was so dark, and the fog was in even thicker, if that were possible, and I was inside Amber, and she breathed hot in my ear. I kissed her neck, her shoulders, her ocean-smelling hair.

After that time neither of us could sleep, thinking of Jamie, so we dressed. Before I could verbalize it, Amber said, "Let's go back to the bay." She looked upon me in a different way, I felt. It was as if we were co-conspirators in some magical game, and then Jamie would . . .

Holding hands, we began the solitary walk back to the bay of the dolphins. Even though a thick fog still shrouded the tiny island and it was black, black out, we sort of knew where to go.

Once back in the bay I began yelling. As loud as my voice would carry, which probably wasn't that far, since sound bounces off the water molecules — fog. And this: the waves were still huge, and we could hear the massive explosions far out in the bay, though we could only see the whitewater that raced up onto the shore.

We walked back and forth in the cove that dark night, shouting Jamie's name, walking back up on the mesa, looking, looking for my friend, Amber's brother. But the fog wouldn't lift, the dawn wouldn't arrive; Jamie did not appear. The waves crashed below and the fog endured. Misty air, breaking waves. Nature. Which had no sentimental cares for our well-being. Alive or dead, nature didn't give a shit. It just kept on going, oblivious to the fact that Jamie was in trouble. Ignorant or cognizant of the fact that Amber and I had hooked up in the midst of all this swirling turmoil. As the guilt intruded, I couldn't help wondering if our having sex ensured the outcome of our island experience. My fault. Amber's and my fault. Bad things happen when you're not married. Jamie must have been right — we shouldn't be together. It did. It didn't. Jamie took that drop of his own free will.

CHAPTER 13

Sometime in the early morning before light I awoke. Seeing the night sky in all its starry glory, I knew a change had occurred. The fog had receded, and I could no longer hear the surf. I lay next to Amber, feeling pangs of love and loss, breathing in the pungent damp island air, listening to the vague night sounds, hearing the gentle surge of the waves in the cove below. I could smell the sea, and smell the chaparral; I could smell Amber, I was permeated with her scent.

She stirred next to me. I breathed in the salt smell of her hair, breathed in her earthy smell, and felt the great glow of desire. And comfort. And dread. My best friend was missing. Amber was beside me. Push pull. High tide low tide. Night day. Male female. Life death.

John Needles. John Needles had lived across the street and over from Jamie. His family and Jamie's family moved in at approximately the same time, since the tract homes were finished at the same time. Jamie hung out with John when they were younger, even though I was always Jamie's best friend. It was just that John was right there, whereas I had to ride a bike over, and wasn't always there, though I was over a lot of the time.

The problem with John Needles was that he liked to see suffering, he liked to throw rocks at cats and liked to taunt dogs in yards and went out of his way to step on snails and in general liked to kill things. I kept my distance from him and so did Jamie, though he was sometimes with us when we did stuff.

When Jamie and I began surfing, John wasn't much interested in it, which was fine with me because I didn't want him down at the beach killing sand crabs and other small sea creatures. Not that he would have been included in the whole deal, but he might have. So the obnoxious neighbor kid was left out.

Until the summer between eighth and ninth grade, when John started surfing. Mrs. Needles came right out and asked Mrs. Watkins if John could come with us to the beach on the mornings she dropped us off. And he did a few times, but by then we were so good, John was embarrassed to surf around us.

So he went on his own to Playa Chica, to areas where there weren't many surfers. Either the waves weren't that big or the shape wasn't good or the tide wasn't right at the places where John surfed on his own. But, still, he surfed, or claimed he did.

I don't know if things would have been different had he been in the water with Jamie and me, but when stuff plays out it's as if there's no way to change the outcome. Like Mr. Watkins's traffic accident. It goes the way it goes.

John Needles was surfing on a spring tide in the afternoon, a huge low tide. He didn't know the sandbars, didn't know the tide was a minus low, a very low tide, probably didn't know enough to bail out behind his board, into the wave, when surfing in shallow water.

That's what I think happened. He fell forward. He ate it in small surf in very shallow water and broke his neck. A beginner long-boarding at Playa Chica and he broke his neck!

The first week after the accident John held his own. Except he was paralyzed from the neck down. Still, there was hope on everyone's part. Jamie and Amber and Mrs. Watkins had all visited him (F might have gone too, because he was in the picture then, acting human), and they said his spirits were good. Even if John Needles tormented animals, you didn't want him to be a quadriplegic.

Yet that's the very thing the doctors told him the beginning of the second week, after they had done a bunch of tests. His spine was messed up, and he wouldn't ever be able to use his arms and legs again. With intensive therapy they might get him to where he could brush his own teeth. Whoopee! It was pretty pathetic, poor John.

He went downhill fast. By the end of the second week after his surfing accident he was gone. Checked out. I only knew about it peripherally, since only his family could visit him at the end. Jamie had gone that one time right after it happened, and then like that it was over.

It was pretty depressing shit, and if John didn't want to hang around as a vegetable, then he was right to check out, if you ask me. But, still, his mother and everyone was torn up. Jamie too. Too close to his father, I guessed. But it passed, though every time I surfed at Playa Chica at low tide I thought of John Needles. I didn't want to think of him.

"You awake?" Amber whispered, bringing me out of my morbid thoughts.

"Yeah."

She snuggled up to my neck, kissing my face. Then she pushed herself away. "You know the thing with Robert? That he was with someone else?"

"Uh huh." I wondered why she wanted to talk about Robert Bonham at this time.

"Well, he wasn't. Not with someone else, I mean. I was."

I lay there looking at the stars, smelling the dew-covered chaparral, thinking, Fuck.

"Don't you want to say anything? Do you want to know about it? Do you want to talk? I think I was trying to drive him away. Maybe I was testing him, I don't know. He's so good."

"Does that mean I'm no good?"

"I don't know anything, Juan."

As I lay there not knowing what to say, I thought I heard the drone of an outboard motor. Distant, far, far away. Tiny and resonant. What do we do? I thought.

"Jesus?" she said.

"I hope so." I pulled her to me, feeling her soft warm curves melt over my chest and knee, and didn't want this moment to end, as Jésus and his boat approached the island.

❧

We were dressed and in the cove by the time it was light enough for the dory to land. Jésus wore a big, I've-saved-you-smile, exuding the optimism of Santiago when he first catches the great fish. He jumped into the shallow water and began pulling his dory onto the sand. I helped him.

"It is so good to see you," I said.

"The swell was so strong I was pushed far south. And then the fog . . ."

"My friend is missing."

"Missing?"

"He was lost in the big waves. Can we search for him in your boat?"

"Of course. Let us go."

First we walked the now familiar route back to the bay. As the sun rose, heat began to infiltrate the island. Amber led, I followed, Jésus bringing up the rear. I watched her walk, pigeon-toed, each foot crossing in front of the other, wearing her cutoff Levi's. I watched her, feeling excitement and emptiness at the same time.

With great anticipation we made our way toward the bay of the dolphins. Once again color permeated everything, and I could see the succulents' fecund drippings and smell the earth and the sea all around us. As we stood above the bay, I was again overwhelmed by its simple beauty. Hundreds of dolphins swam below our perch up on the dunes. The shape of the waves was still good, and they were substantial, though only breaking on the inside reef, I knew. From up here, we could see that nobody, no human was in the water; our boards were still on the sand were we'd left them.

We dropped down to the beach, walking to the far point. I climbed the mound so that I could see into the next cove — nothing. No board, no footprints, no waves, even. The bottom wasn't right, I supposed. "Nothing here!" I shouted to them.

When I got back on the beach I could see Amber's eyes were red-rimmed. "It's possible he's in another cove. He paddled out of the bay, and then the current swept him farther away."

I said this to Jésus as well. He agreed and said he knew the direction the current would take somebody.

So we made our way back to the landing cove, where we'd camped. Once back in the dory after loading our stuff, we began a long, fruitless search for Jamie. We motored to various coves, Jésus speculating on wind and tide currents, guessing where a surfer on his board in outrageous swells and shrouded in fog might end up. We drifted off the island; we landed in coves that faced different directions from the bay of the dolphins, combing the beaches for any sign of Jamie. In the early afternoon, exhausted and listless, we motored into the dreamlike bay of the dolphins. Ocean mammals surrounded our boat, chattering and flopping and jumping into the air.

I dove in the water, and swam down, down, down, until I could touch the flat reef rocks. It was hard to see, but I swam around, hoping to catch a glimpse of something. Two dolphins swam with me, watching every move I made, their muzzles close. Suddenly the dolphins skittered away, and then Amber was beside me, our eyes open underwater, and in the gathering dark we were surrounded by more and more returning dolphins. Then we had to surface.

We searched and searched for Jamie around the island; we landed in strange coves, walked on beaches that probably had never had another human on them. We dove in bays that had sandy bottoms, we dove in bays that had jagged rock bottoms, we dove in one bay that had a bunch of sharks in it, but we didn't know until we were in the water. Jésus showed me how to track the ocean current that led away from the island, and we followed it some distance off its shore. Jamie was nowhere. Disappeared off the planet.

Jésus said he was running low on fuel and that we would have to get back to the mainland. Amber and I didn't feel like staying on the island either, so we motored back to Ensenada Harbor, arriving in the early morning hours, before light, amidst the bustle of the fishermen unloading their catches and swampers hosing out stalls in the fish market.

We were dazed, in a surreal dream in which things just wouldn't go back to "right." But, still, we had to go through the motions. And we did. We would head back home, and tell our parents. They would help us find Jamie because he was still there, of that I was positive.

CHAPTER 14

I was arrested at the border. After an hour in the chaotic traffic line of time-stop darting cars moving from one nonexistent lane to another. Past times I'd joked with the souvenir sellers, even once bought a velvet Jesus dripping velvet blood at velvet Golgotha. This time, Amber and I just suffered in silence the boredom of moving forward inch by inch, thinking about the unknown fate that awaited our return. What would we say to our parents? To friends? Jamie was missing.

I'd assumed that we'd return without him — that was the original plan; he'd be settled at my aunt's trailer, or in a motel at the least, safe. Amber and I would return. Jamie would come back when things blew over at home.

We couldn't even find his board. Any time I closed my eyes I saw that mammoth wave, saw Jamie take the drop, saw him airborne, saw his rooster tail after he disappeared in that barrel, and then no longer saw his path on the wave any longer. After that everything becomes hazy. Mostly re-creations not necessarily based upon fact.

I don't remember Amber getting me out of the water. Don't remember the savior dolphin. Don't really remember riding the entire night in Jésus's dinghy out beyond the bay, searching, yelling, shining flashlights onto black fast-moving water.

Hindus say that this life is but a dream. Maybe everything that happened was a dream. Maybe Amber and I had run off to celebrate our new relationship. Maybe Jamie would be home, worried about Amber and me, the same as everyone else.

Silent the whole way, Amber refused to drive no matter how much I asked, and I didn't have good feeling because of it. I wouldn't beg, though. It was as if Tijuana reminded her of our carefree actions, and now we had to pay the consequences for them. "Beware your friend," Half-man on Skateboard had warned me. At the time I thought he was referring to Amber.

When it was our turn to be interrogated by the Border Patrol agent, I stopped my mother's 4Runner next to the little booth, with a bad feeling in my gut and a sinking heart. It had been hot and dry while waiting in the endless lines to reach this point, but now, under the postmodern arch that sheltered all the re-entry bays, it was shady and breezy, almost cool. I wished we had just walked across, but that wasn't happening. Besides, the car . . .

"Citizenship?" the border cop asked.

"U.S."

"Citizenship, miss?" he asked when Amber didn't respond.

She still didn't answer, only twirled Jamie's sunglasses. She put them on. I could see tears on her cheek.

"Do you have a problem? Can you not speak?" the agent said.

"She's U.S., sir," I said.

"I asked her."

"She's upset."

"I can see that. What are you bringing with you from Mexico that you wish to declare?"

"Nothing."

"Will you please both step out of the car?"

I exited the car on the driver's side. Amber remained seated. Leaning into the window, I said, "You're blowing it, Amber."

She said nothing. She looked straight ahead, Jamie's aviator sunglasses obscuring her face.

The cop walked around the car, looking in all the windows, looking at our boards and clothes, at the general disarray of our things.

Amber took off the sunglasses and began fidgeting with them, finally setting them on the driver's seat.

When the agent stood in front of me, he poked me hard in the waist with his flashlight. He wore black leather gloves, and they gripped his steel flashlight with authority.

"Hey!" I said, recoiling.

He paid me no mind, opening the car door, reaching under the seats, poking around. He stood up, outside the car, and seemed to notice for the first time Jamie's glasses on the seat. He leaned forward, putting his hand right on the glasses, breaking them while he looked under the front seat another time. He gave Amber a hard look and then one to me. I gazed in the asshole's eyes, not blinking.

He walked around to Amber's side of the car and told her to get out. She just sat there, looking at the glasses. He went back to his little booth and made a phone call. When he came back he went straight for Amber, opening the door and pulling her out. Amber resisted, becoming dead weight. Once he had her out, he searched under the seats for whatever it was he looked for. While he was bent over, Amber kicked him in the ass.

He was a big man with a crew cut, and I didn't think he could move quickly, or with such agile grace, but he did. He was on Amber in a heartbeat, pinning both her arms behind her back, pushing her toward the office on the right side of the bays.

"Wait!" I yelled, taking off after them. Before I'd taken two steps I found myself on the ground with a knee in my back and my hands pinned behind, cuffed.

❧

"Tell me your story again," the man said. He was some sort of detective for the DEA, and he thought that Amber and I were smuggling drugs. I'd told him the truth, the whole story, but he believed that Jamie was following us, with the drugs. He stuck to his scenario, and nothing I said could disabuse him from that notion. Because of his belief, my mother's car was entirely torn apart: side door panels off and on the ground next to it; headliner shredded and the pieces lying on the ground as if a windstorm had blasted through the car's interior; air filter and other engine bolt-ons spread out over the ground; Greg Scott's sleeping bags ripped apart, flung on the cement with the other objects. I could see all this through the interrogation room window. They'd wanted me to watch them destroy my mother's car, probably hoping I'd come clean rather than have the car damaged, but I had nothing to offer other than the truth, which was something this man had no use for.

"Just let me call my parents," I said for the umpteenth time.

148

The man was old, probably in his forties, fit, with a thin mustache and large ears. His hair was short and dark. He wore a suit and tie. "Why did your friend attack a United States agent?"

"She didn't attack him. She kicked him in the ass because he broke her brother's sunglasses on purpose."

"That hardly warrants a federal charge, does it?"

"She's upset. Her brother's missing."

"Yes, that's right, so you claim." He cracked his gum and rolled it between his upper teeth and lower teeth.

"That's right."

"On this island."

"Yeah."

"Where is the island again?"

"I already told you."

"Tell me again."

"South and west of Ensenada."

"That's right. And what's its name?"

"C'mon. Aren't you bored? I am."

"Just tell me again the name of the island."

"La Isla de Los Delfíns."

"Why isn't it on any maps?"

(We would find out much later that Jésus had used the common name for the island; the proper name, of course, was on the map.)

"I wouldn't know."

I looked at the man who interrogated me. He sat in a chair with a back and armrests. On the table he had a stained coffee cup with a big chip on the lip. He also had an endless supply of gum, which he chewed with abandon.

"I find your entire story odd. I think your friend, the one who's supposed to be missing, has drugs. I think you and his sister were going to meet him along the barrier, where you would then place the drugs in that car and he would join you. You're going to tell me your meeting place."

"I want to call my parents."

"You're a car thief. The car you were driving was reported stolen. You have no rights. I don't care how many television shows you've watched, you're nothing here, okay? You don't get shit unless I okay it. Understand?"

I sighed. I knew his drug theory, but hadn't known that my mother's car was reported. "Yes, sir."

"Where are you meeting your friend?"

I'm not sure, I thought.

CHAPTER 15

I sat on a long bench in front of an institution-green picnic table, my mother across from me on its counterpart. I couldn't look her in the eye. She was dressed for work, hair done with hairspray, jewelry that was simple yet stylish, and a pantsuit and low heels. My father was so angry that he wouldn't come. Evidently my mother had taken the train to San Diego to get me out. I was held in a detention center for juveniles, a ward of the San Diego Sheriff's Department. I'd been arrested for grand theft auto, and my experience so far was nothing like the game!

My mother told me she had reported the car stolen before she realized that I was gone, otherwise she might not have done so. She wasn't sure. At any rate, the damage was done.

In a big empty room my mother was the only other human, if you didn't count the burly guard who blocked the only door. After being in the hands of law-enforcement people, I was wondering whether or not some of them were human. Many of them were like pit bulls; once something was in their mind, that was it, end of story, fuck you. For some people reality and truth have nothing to do with anything. I realized that those kinds of people exist everywhere, but it just seemed that there was a disproportionate number of them associated with my incarceration.

"Why didn't you come to us?" my mother said.

I wanted to say, "You're really crabby when awakened," but said only, "We didn't want to bother you." I couldn't tell her about the approaching swell, our expectations of big waves, good surf, a perfect wave. That was just too selfish.

"You did get my message, right?"

"Oh, yes, we heard you. Why . . . ?" she broke off, looking away toward the ground. When her gaze came back to me she said, "And you're sure about Jamie? You're not lying?"

I looked onto the hard, cold cement floor. There was an old wad of chewing gum hard-melted into a white spot. Suddenly my nose burned, and I tried not to cry.

"Okay, sorry," she said, turning away and dabbing her eyes. "But, I mean, you didn't have to run away."

"We thought Jamie was going to get arrested."

"He might have. But that's better than what happened, isn't it?"

I looked at my mother. She looked tired, and for the first time I thought of what she must have been like when she was young. I'll bet she would have helped her friend out; I'll bet she would have. "So what happens now?"

"I'm not sure. Jamie injured Frederick. He's in the hospital."

"But F attacked him."

"Use his proper name, please. I know what you kids call him."

"Whatever. Anyway, Jamie was attacked. He just defended himself."

"That's not for us to sort out. When did Jamie get so mean?"

"He's *not* mean! Not at all."

"When did he turn so hard?"

"He didn't, Mom; stuff just kept happening to him."

We sat in silence, the huge bureaucratic building ticking with a life of its own. The building and all the pit bulls still hadn't found Jamie.

"Where's Amber? Can she come back with us?"

"She's been released."

"When?"

"I don't know. These people aren't exactly forthcoming with their information. And I haven't talked with Claire." And then with no segue, "Are you hungry?"

I still had no appetite, even though I'd not eaten in God knows how long. "No, Mom, they fed me." I wondered what she meant about Claire not speaking with her, but said nothing.

"I'm seeing a bondsman in awhile. He'll try to get you out before the weekend, but he may not be able to, since it's Friday. He'll do his best. I'll do my best."

"I understand, Mom. I'm so sorry." And after thinking on it for a moment, I said, "Are there charges against Jamie?" We might be in the same boat.

"I don't know."

After my mother left I was transferred to another part of the compound, the drunk tank. With adults. Men. Drunk men. I supposed it was to teach me a lesson. Seeing all those drunk guys coming in hour after hour, vomiting on the floor, on themselves, on anyone who was close to them, was disgusting. The stench was enough to make a sober person vomit, and I dry-heaved, but there was nothing in my stomach. Was I drunk when I stole my mother's car? Was I drunk to help my friend?

Finally I was released in the early evening, and my mother and I drove north. She didn't stop, except for gas, and the only comment she made about her formerly new and now torn-up 4Runner was to gasp upon seeing it.

I'd imagined the Border Patrol agents might put everything back together — you know, put the side panels on, try to put back the headliner. But no, they'd piled everything in the back of the car, a constant reminder of my criminal status, and how I'd dragged my family into it.

❧

"What were you thinking?" Raul said. He stood in his former room, my room now, leaning against the dresser. Even though I sort of reveled in my bittersweet privacy, I missed my brother a lot. I'd seen him every day of my life, and now the only way I could hang out with him was if I stopped by his apartment. But he was never home because he worked a full-time job.

"I guess I wasn't, not really. It just seemed like the cool thing to do. I didn't want Jamie to get in trouble, and things just kept happening." Now I was the one arrested!

My brother had done his share of shit, but nothing that could compare with the mess I was in. "But stealing the car? Jamie drowned? You're not covering for him?"

As the bridge of my nose got edgy and my vision clouded I fought back the tears. "He didn't drown!"

"Okay," he said in a softer voice.

My mother was making a big Sunday meal and had invited my brother and his wife over. Bonnie, who was just starting to show in her pregnancy, was in the kitchen talking with my mother.

"How come there's no island on the map?"

"I don't know." Did I dream Jésus? Did I dream the wave Jamie took off on? Had I only dreamed my nights with Amber? "It's really weird."

"Maybe not," he said. "Maybe only the fishermen know about it. Maybe they don't want people to know where it is. The simple thing would be to find that fisherman again, that's all."

"Yeah," I said. "Jamie's there. I know he is. Would you take me back?"

My brother just stared at me. We looked alike, the same brown hair, the same long black eyelashes, the same lean profile, though I was more developed in my upper body from surfing all the time. He cared about his clothes, I didn't.

Before he could answer, my mother called us to dinner and we left the safety of the room. It was no-man's-land for me in the house anywhere my father was. Nestor was pissed off big time but couldn't do much right now because Jamie was missing.

At the table I let Bonnie sit in my seat, my brother took his old seat next to her, and my little sister and brother sat across from them. I was seated next to my mother, who sat at the opposite end of the table from my father. I wanted to be as far from him as possible. On a collapsible chair and using a corner to set my plate, I tried to eat.

Nestor started to dig in but my mother made him stop. "We're going to say grace from now on," she announced.

My father looked at her oddly. "I don't think so."

"I think yes," she said with all her female authority. "In fact, I think this family should start going to church on a regular basis again."

Oh, God, what havoc have I wreaked on my poor family?

My brother and Bonnie smirked, but my mother led us in grace, thanking the Lord for my return, and hoping that Jamie found everlasting peace.

"Stop acting like he's dead," I said. "He's still down there."

"Let it go," my mother said in her soft and quiet way.

"No."

"You stop this crap!" my father said.

I didn't want to cry in front of Bonnie or anything, so I ran outside in the backyard, where I climbed on the block wall and looked toward the ocean. There was no swell, the wind was blowing hard, and I sat on the wall with the sea breeze all around me, thinking how odd things had turned out.

I was facing a felony charge of auto theft. Because of bail I was under some sort of house arrest; I couldn't leave without parental supervision, and as far as my father was concerned I could rot in the house. I was grounded until I was eighteen, I figured. He still hadn't talked to me. Just ignored or yelled at me.

Amber was in Oklahoma with relatives. Robert Bonham had gone with her, I heard. Robert Bonham picked her up in San Diego too. Greg Scott had told me. He came by, and so had Herbie and Ricky, a few of the guys I surfed with. Just to hear the story. The lawyer my parents hired was trying to cut a deal so that I would be charged with a misdemeanor, with probation. So far the D.A. had resisted. I was not to contact Amber, but couldn't since I didn't know where she was.

And F? F was fucked up. Some brain damage or something. His beating precipitated a stroke or something, something so that his brain didn't get enough oxygen, and he was major fucked. He was still in the hospital, though it was for therapy now, and not because he was in any danger. And Claire wouldn't talk with any of my family. Greg Scott heard that she blamed me for everything that happened. But I didn't make F attack Jamie, and I didn't make Jamie give F brain damage, of that I'm sure. Besides, when Jamie returns he'll set things straight

I wondered what he was up to? How could he survive on that island? And how would he be after going through all that stuff alone? We had to get back to him, somehow. Somehow I'd have to find him.

Inside the house I could hear the quiet buzz of conversation as my family continued with the meal. Let nothing stop the meal! Not the fact that my best friend was still on an island down in Mexico, not the fact that I haven't seen Amber, not the fact that I may face a trial and so could Jamie when he returns. Let the meal go forward! Life goes on.

CHAPTER 16

We didn't have to run, I know now. In fact, stealing my mother's car and running away were about the stupidest things I hoped I'd ever do. I was facing a felony charge, Amber wasn't around, Jamie was still in Mexico, and I would *not* return to school until he was found. I just couldn't face it. My English teacher, Mr. Vance, who was also my homeroom teacher, immediately enrolled me in SISE, an acronym for Short-term Independent Study Education. I got my work every day from Greg Scott, and sent back the previous day's work with him.

Until things were resolved regarding Jamie and my pending case, I refused to go back to school. The only way it worked with Nestor was because I had told my mom that I just couldn't bear to return without Jamie, that I couldn't face the other kids' knowing what I had done. And it worked; she was sympathetic and argued my case to Nestor.

For a brief time I was a person of interest with law enforcement regarding Jamie's disappearance. And for a time, a very short time, there was some interest in the story in the local newspaper, where I was an unnamed participant whose name was withheld because of age. But as the newspaper interest had faded, so had the notion that I had somehow been involved in foul play regarding Jamie's disappearance. They — some detectives — interviewed everybody in sight, even Greg Scott and some of the other guys who were on the beach the day that F attacked Jamie. Everybody knew I couldn't have done anything bad to Jamie.

The D.A. was holding off my trial date until there was some break regarding Jamie's disappearance. They had been hoping they could charge me with something more serious, my lawyer speculated. Part of the problem was that nobody had jurisdiction over how to find Jamie. Since I was arrested at the border by Homeland Security and then transferred to the San Diego Sheriff's Department, technically they — the Sheriff's Department — had the jurisdiction if a crime were committed. But no crime had been committed in San Diego County, so they didn't care. And back in my county, the crime that had been committed was GTA, which I was charged with. Both the D.A. and my lawyer were waiting for something to break regarding Jamie. But it had to come from the Mexican authorities, who didn't seem much to care about it, for nothing ever seemed to come of the inquiries made on Jamie's behalf, or so we heard.

My lawyer told us that the D.A. was trying to make inquiries with the Mexican Consulate and the U.S. State Department. But due to perpetually underfunded bureaucracies, the ball had dropped, so to speak.

I just missed my friend and wanted him back.

At some point our lawyer suggested that my parents hire a private detective or a bounty hunter to go down there and find Jamie (what he meant was proof of Jamie's drowning), but when the cost was presented, my parents declined. They didn't have that kind of money. My mother told the lawyer to contact Claire Watkins about the possibility, but he said she wouldn't return his calls.

Every time I saw my brother I worked on him to take me back down, but he couldn't — his wife was pregnant and he thought it would be uncool to leave her at this time, and he had a full-time job, which he couldn't lose. I saw his point, sort of.

But one day at lunch he showed up just to see me. "I've got Bimbo Burgers," he said.

"Cool." He brought me three of the little cheeseburgers, fries, and a chocolate shake.

"I know you're on house arrest," he said, unwrapping his regular-sized hamburger and taking a big bite. He had a Diet Coke, no fries. "But Nestor won't let you surf?"

"Naw, he'd like to kill me, if he could."

"Don't say that."

"It's true."

"You did mess up. I mean, really!"

He looked right at me and smiled. I missed my brother. He didn't surf and he didn't play any sports; he really came alive when he danced though, even going on TV dance shows years ago. Back then he danced on weekend nights at the local hip-hop clubs too. I was too young to get in those places. Amber had been a few times with Robert Bonham, but she was really too young to go as well. She had said everyone was drinking, and I knew my brother had too, because I could hear him bumping into things when he came home late at night when we still shared a room. Now he was gone, married to his high school girlfriend, Bonnie. My sister-in-law. She was cool. But, still, my brother was gone. It was a weird situation. My parents weren't really happy that he'd gotten his girlfriend pregnant.

After we inhaled the food and while he was crumpling the wrappers and placing them back in the bag, he said, "I just thought I'd see how you're doing. I don't see you much anymore."

I nodded my head in agreement. "You know, we could go back down and look for Jamie some weekend. It would only take a couple of days. We could find him, I know we could."

While standing up, he looked down at the table. "I'm sorry, I can't. Shit, what time is it? I've got to pick up Bonnie at the doctor's." He looked sort of sad, and older.

✧

As the weeks wore on, I had to enroll in LISE, the acronym for Long-term Independent Study Education. For major fuckups. Kids who were expelled or convicted of drug crimes and violent crimes. I had to go to the continuation high school once a week to get my work, my mother dropping me off and picking me up. Since I didn't know any of those kids, it was no big deal. My work would be checked (it was always excellent), and I could do as many assignments as I wanted. The teachers seemed to think it was a big deal that my science labs were dry, but I didn't care. I didn't much like dissecting things and mixing stuff anyway. Besides, I was way ahead of the expectations for what I should do per week, months ahead really, because there wasn't anything else to do, and I was never a huge television watcher, and I was banned from online stuff and everything else, so why not do the schoolwork, keep up with my class?

Except Mrs. Perez, my counselor, said my missing the tenth grade would have dire consequences for my college application process. So would a felony, I told her.

One afternoon I was just sitting around after doing my schoolwork. My father was asleep and my mother was at work and my little brother and sister were in school. I just felt like getting out of the house, and though I wasn't supposed to, I walked all the way to the Albertson's on the back end of the mesa. It was close to Halloween, and I always liked to look at all the candy in the stores. The candy reminded me of when I used to trick-or-treat, reminded me of all the candy we used to eat, and the fun I had running door to door with Jamie and our friends.

A strong Santa Ana wind was blowing, bending the eucalyptus trees and the huge cypress trees that bordered the mesa from when it used to be farmland and the trees were functional, windbreaks. I could see forever, see the mountains that ringed the huge basin where we lived, could even see the granite white rocks on the top of the highest mountain, which made it look as if it had snow on it, even though it was over eighty degrees out. It felt so good to be out of doors, to be away from my house where it seemed as if I were under house arrest, which I was, if Nestor had his way. When I looked back over my shoulder, I could see the ocean all whitecapped and blustery-looking.

My family had lived on this mesa above Playa Chica for a number of generations. Behind the mesa was the Colonia, the barrio where some of my relatives lived. My great-grandfather had had the foresight to buy property on the mesa when it was inexpensive. My grandfather had built our house there after World War II when it was affordable to build. Only people who wanted horses and land with neighbors far removed had purchased at that time, and things had pretty much remained the same, except that our house was old. As I looked at it now it seemed sort of shabby next to the newer, bigger homes.

Walking in the market, I remembered the Halloween when Jamie had brought his father's duffle bag, and wouldn't stop trick-or-treating until it was halfway filled with candy. I smiled looking at all those bags of Snickers, my favorite, and M&M's and Peanut Butter Cups, everything piled up in a huge square right when you walked in, like the farmers' market for candy, the horn of plenty for rotting your teeth. I was thinking of treating myself to a bag when I saw something that shook me up so much I forgot about candy.

I saw F. He was on his own in the market, using a walker. He shuffled along like an old man. Seeing him like that gave me goose bumps and I ran all the way home.

As I stood inside the entry hall in our house, I heard Nestor coming down the hallway. I was breathing hard so I flopped down on the floor and began doing push-ups.

"What are you doing?" Nestor said. It looked as if he'd just gotten out of the shower.

"I can't get any other form of exercise," I said.

"You can go to school."

Before I could think of a comeback, Paul burst in saying, "Hi, Dad!"

They went into the kitchen to get snacks. I went to my room.

Seeing F like that brought to mind what my mother had said about Jamie. For some reason I couldn't get her comments that Jamie was mean and hard out of my head. Both of those words were pretty bad for her to say. She meant that he was a lout, an unsavory character, in her opinion. I had never heard her use such harsh terms regarding any of my friends, and I couldn't let it go.

Why would she think that of Jamie?

He'd always been my friend, and sure, we got in a few spats over Monopoly and ball games, one accusing the other of cheating, or one of us just pissed off over losing, whatever, nothing serious. Nothing that had ever come close to blows.

Maybe she meant the change that had come over him after his father died. He had changed so much over those years. It wasn't quick or anything, something very gradual and subtle, as I thought about it. Something that my mother could spot out after knowing Jamie for so many years, since he was practically a baby. She could see the change, maybe when I couldn't.

But that he was mean and hard? What's hard? If she meant that he's tough, can fight well, then that's right. So what?

The Kent Chambers fight had come to him, and so had every one of the others, if I remembered right. In fact, one time a guy punched Jamie right in the jaw, and he just looked at the guy in passing. It was for no reason, when we were at the pier at night, and walking back through the parking lot to head over to some-body's house. We passed some older, drunk guys, and one of them hauled off and hit Jamie. It staggered him for a second, and I thought I saw his knees buckle just the slightest, but then he kept on walking without missing a beat. I think it had been around the Fourth of July or something, a time when it's full-party-drunk-out-time at the beach and inland assholes are ubiquitous.

And there was another time when Aaron Stangy tried to pick a fight because Jamie wouldn't loan him his board. Aaron was a hog, a leech, one of those guys who liked to surf but never seemed to have a board of his own. He'd always borrow boards from kooks and shit.

Jamie hadn't fought him, either.

But then I remembered the time we were skateboarding in front of Jamie's house, and John Needles was still around then, the three of us just grinding off the curb and stuff, talking and hanging out on a Friday night. Some other kids came by, kids we didn't know, and mouthed off. There were like five of them.

Jamie just went at the biggest one and kicked his ass. Pretty fast. That's how most fights were, a bunch of flailing fists and arms and sometimes legs, and one guy would get tagged, and the other guy would go in for the kill. A guy might get hit in the face or something, and see his own blood and freak out, or get energized or something and go off one way or the other. I think Jamie broke the guy's nose on the first punch, because there was a lot of blood and the guy seemed unable to see, and Jamie just wiped the floor with him, shutting up those other boys as they took off helping their friend. There were a number of fights from confrontations in the water too. And one on the beach not long ago when a guy was trying to break into Claire's car. Jamie had taken it, of course, without her permission. He beat the crap out of that guy too. But I always thought Jamie was in the right in all his fights. But did he *have* to fight, I guess was the question. To look at it through my mother's eyes, I'd have to answer that question. And I could see now from more perspective that, no, he didn't always have to fight. Kent Chambers had made him fight. And F had made him fight Kent Chambers the second time. But there were others after and before when he truly didn't have to.

As I thought about it, I realized I was always half-afraid that Jamie was going to go off on someone, especially when we surfed. I thought it was just the way things were in the water. But not everyone is like that. Lots of guys surf without ever getting in fights. Certainly not fights in the water. Maybe Jamie was different. Maybe he did have a penchant for violence in the same way that I had a blind spot for him and ignored his violent tendencies. But when you grow up with a guy, a guy who's your best friend, you tend to overlook certain things. Perhaps I was wrong to do so. Possibly that was what my mother was saying.

I couldn't answer my mother's indictment one way or the other. On some level she was right, maybe. But there were other considerations.

And the one that I couldn't answer, ever, was the one about losing his father. That was a perspective that I couldn't get into, no matter how hard I tried. And I hoped I would never have to, for the prospect seemed too horrible. Nestor pisses me off sometimes, but he's my father, end of story.

Jamie lost his father. And he was never the same.

But could the stuff with F have gone differently? Did Jamie have to fight and injure F? Could he have just gotten out of there, and possibly the police would have dealt with F? I don't know, and I'll never know because the fight had escalated, and Jamie had done what he was very good at: fight.

∽

My mother had threatened our family with church, and she kept her word. Two weekends after my "transgression" — my mother's term for stealing her car and running away with Jamie and Amber to Mexico on a surf trip — we went back to mass as a family.

Week after week we had to endure the monotone priest, the beaming parishioners, the handshakes at the end followed by "Peace be with you." One Sunday as I sat in the pew between Nestor and Paul, I remembered the times Raul and I used to ride our bikes to early mass. So that we would be finished with the obligation early enough to get on with our day: He would hook up with a girlfriend, I would surf. What I remembered was getting the giggles (we always sat in the very back of the not-very-filled church) when Raul would stuff trash in the collection envelope, or gum, or even snot once. I would imagine some officious layperson opening the envelope. . . .

I must have chuckled, for Paul slugged me in the arm. I leaned down and whispered, "Love, Jesus," while pinching the baby fat under his ribs.

He shrieked, and everyone in the whole congregation looked at us. Nestor spoke in a hushed though severe voice to him, and then glared at me. What, was I going to get in more trouble? I didn't give a shit, if this was my life.

I figured I *would* get in trouble big time from Nestor once we got home, but the opposite happened. He was so impatient to leave that he took off before the priest walked down the aisle with the incense and shit he carried. My mother was furious with Nestor, almost running to catch him as we hustled to the gravel subsidiary parking lot, the overflow lot, where we were forced to park, since we'd arrived late. My mother liked to hang out in front of the church after mass, exchanging pleasantries with strangers. Once she caught up to him she said, "What kind of example do you think you're setting for your children?"

"What?" Nestor said. "I want to go."

"What's the big rush?"

"I don't want to get stuck in the logjam getting out. This parking lot's a bottleneck. We'll be here a half hour."

"So what?"

Before I'd even buckled my seat belt, Nestor peeled out, spraying gravel as he lurched the car toward the exit.

"That's it!" my mother shouted. "You're not going next week. You're banned."

I thought I saw Nestor crack the slightest grin as I looked at his face in the rearview mirror.

❧

The first therapist I had to see was a therapist-in-training, and she was free, available from my church, St. Mary's. My mother had talked to Father Daniels, and he suggested that I begin sessions with Ms. Catrone.

The first session we just met and I pretty much wouldn't talk. Why should I speak with a stranger? Why should I pour out my heart to someone I didn't know? I didn't. And when I did talk in the few sessions we had, I withheld the good stuff. I said that F was a cheap jerk and that Jamie should be given a medal for fucking him up. Ms. Catrone didn't think I was being very charitable. It was hard to reconcile the image of F in the market with the one of him dragging Jamie off the beach that day. But the violent image always won out, ergo my apathy toward what had happened to F.

She wanted me to talk about my feelings about Amber, once I said that we'd hooked up. But I wasn't going to tell that woman anything about her. Talking about it would somehow lessen our experience, wouldn't it?

She knew we weren't getting anywhere so she cut off my sessions. She told my parents that I didn't trust her, which was true, I supposed. And it was fine because there was nothing wrong with me; I was just stalling until Jamie returned. They'd find him, or he'd simply get back on his own somehow. Jamie could do it, I just knew he could.

I had a fantasy about Jamie returning one day, all scraggly, like Chance, Shadow, and Fluffy had done in *The Incredible Journey*. There'd be so much celebrating that the whole area wouldn't be able to contain itself, not the teachers at my high school or continuation school, not any of the law-enforcement people, not the D.A. or my lawyer, not the neighbors who now looked at us askance; not anyone, we'd all be so happy that all the bad stuff would go away.

❦

"Don't you know anyone who drives?" I said. Greg Scott and I were sitting in my room after school was out for him.

"Robert Bonham." Greg Scott thought he was funny.

"You're not funny, dude," I snarled at him. "I want to go back down."

"You can't, dude. You're on bail." He was sitting on my bed playing his newest handheld.

"So?"

"So, you jump bail and they send bounty hunters after *you.*"

I knew he was right. But it was just that months were going by and nothing had happened. Except that Amber wasn't coming back, I didn't think, and Claire had separated from F, or so we heard.

"Would your dad take us?"

"Shit, man, I got so much heat for getting you guys the sleeping bags and stuff. Gimme a break." He turned off his system. "You know who's dating Corinna now?"

I had had a crush on her since the fourth grade. Now, after Amber, Corinna Cervantes seemed a little girl. "No, who?"

"Dan Avon." Greg looked at me as if I were supposed to care. I didn't. "Don't you think it's kind of weird?"

"Why?" I couldn't care less who went out with Corinna.

"You don't seem to care about much these days," Greg said, putting his things in his backpack, getting ready to go home, I guessed.

He was right, I didn't.

"Let's check out the waves," Greg said.

We went into my backyard and climbed up on the block wall. Not much was going on in the ocean.

"When do you get to surf again?" Greg Scott said.

"Ask Nestor."

After he left I felt so lonely I thought I might actually cry, the one thing everyone was trying to get me to do, but also the thing I refused to do. Jamie was coming back. . . .

❧

And Amber, well, I was now almost embarrassed about how I'd behaved. Not for anything I'd done. More so for how I felt. I was nothing to her. No, that's not true either. I just wasn't Robert Bonham; nobody could be, I now saw. They were meant for each other, I think, and I got in the way for a time. A very short time. I guess like the other guy she had fooled around with. Why would I think she would want to be my girlfriend?

It's so silly, even though I have these incredible dreams about her. Last night we were in the ocean and I started kissing her and we were getting down to business, and when I opened my eyes underwater Amber was a dolphin, pulling me into a wave in the dream. Almost all the dreams are about sex and we don't quite do it, or are interrupted or otherwise thwarted. But in the dreams she still wants to, and I guess that's something.

I guess we connect with people in so many different ways; there are so many different forms of like and love and friendship. I'm good friends with Greg Scott, but he's not Jamie and never will be. But he's got my back and he does everything that a friend can do, and vice versa on my part. And there are other guys as well. Girls too. Girls who just seem to like me because I'm me, not any going-out stuff.

172

Maybe I should care that Corinna likes that fool Dan Avon. Maybe I should let her know that I liked her for a long time. Or it can wait; it's waited long enough. I guess the big thing is that I see that I could hook up with someone else again, and I don't begrudge Amber's being with the person she wants to be with.

CHAPTER 17

All winter the coast was battered by El Niño storms. Huge weather systems from the gulf of Alaska generating massive swells that hit our coastline. Wind and rain pelted the house, flooding the streets and closing Pacific Coast Highway on a weekly basis. And I couldn't surf. I stayed around the house doing schoolwork, talking with friends on the phone, and seeing Greg Scott on the weekends. My lawyer stalled the courts, and sucked money from my parents.

Robert Bonham showed up one rainy afternoon and knocked on the door.

"What do you want?"

"Amber's board."

"No way!" I snarled.

"We're getting married. I thought you'd want to know."

"Fuck you." I pushed him off the porch, out into the rain. When he came back at me I slammed the door and locked it.

He pounded on the door and then kicked it. "You're lucky I don't kick your ass, you little asshole. She's marrying me!" he yelled through the closed front door.

I stood quiet in the hall, until I slid down the wall and sat on the cold damp tiles. I could see the television set from where I sat, and couldn't help remembering a time when Amber had showed up at the front door, breathless and in need.

And they did marry.

Amber sent me a letter, one that's creased slick from having been read so many times, I could see as I looked at it yet again.

Dearest Juan,

By now you must know I'm married to Robert. Please, please, please forgive me if I have hurt you.

I can't explain what happened down in Mexico with us, all that happened on the island. I still don't know what to make of it. But I know you're a part of my life in the same way that Jamie is a part of me. You were my brother's dearest, closest friend. I miss you. I miss Jamie. Oh, how I miss Jamie. And you must too. It must be so very hard for you, Juan. I hope hearing from me doesn't make things even worse. My intention is to ease your mind, to tell you that I'm okay, I'm getting on, that you are always in my heart, and I hope that I might see you someday.

Much love,
Amber

P.S.: My mother's wrong to hold anything against you. You acted, you didn't hesitate to help Jamie. She will realize that someday.

Claire did hold me responsible, my mother told me. She, Claire, had told my mother when they finally spoke that had it not been for me, her son would be alive. My mother told her that she, Claire, was the person most responsible, if there were blame to lay, which there wasn't. They talked no more after that. And my life was completely severed from that of the Watkinses.

❧

As the winter wore on into early spring, and the first peach trees blossomed and then the apricots followed, my thoughts began to change. I knew that Jamie was not coming back. This was a result of everyone pounding that fact into my head, everyone from the parish priest to the court-appointed counselor I now had to see once a week. My father, my mother, my older brother, Amber in her letter, all of these things.

And this: even though I wasn't to leave the house, one day I got my bike from the garage and rode over to Jamie's. It was sort of far, and would take too long to walk before my father awoke. I wanted to confront Claire. Why wouldn't she talk with me, or see me? She never even asked anything about why we left, or what had happened to Jamie. I wanted to ask her, Why did Amber have to be in Oklahoma, married? Of course I wasn't to have contact with any of the Watkins family, but she could have at least called or something. But she hadn't.

A strong onshore breeze blew all the eucalyptus trees that lined the mesa's northern edge. When I looked back I could see the ocean all dark and stormy, whitecaps luffing along the sea's edge. I crossed Golden Sunset Street, entering Jamie's housing tract, pedaling on autopilot the different streets to his house. Jamie should be there; what if he were there? I think I just wanted to see Claire, who was a Watkins, after all.

On the ride over I remembered when Robert Bonham had entered the scene. He was a Sheila magnet, a very good surfer, popular in school, so I was told. Or overheard when Amber was squealing into her phone to one of her friends. Robert had asked her out, she said over and over. Robert would hold no water with the slutty girls.

Around that time Jamie never wanted to do anything other than sleep or hang in his room. I made him at least throw grounders in the backyard. And Amber's bedroom window was always open so I could hear her phone conversations. I could hear her excitement, which made me happy for her. Once for me the Watkins house was the house of mirth; then it was the palace of denial. Jamie would just go through the motions like he was sleepwalking or something, many of the balls just dribbling under his legs and he didn't give a shit. I'd have to go get the ball and throw it to him again.

"Yeah, can you believe it?" Amber yelled in the phone. "Friday! My mom said yes! I don't know! Yeah! Yeah!"

And so it went. I figured it was a big deal for a bunch of reasons. Robert Bonham was a stud, a player, a guy with a car who could have his pick of girls. He was in the eleventh grade, Amber in the ninth at that time. He was an older guy. But he could see Amber's qualities even though she was young. A lot of guys talked to her and talked about her but not many asked her out. And of the few who did, she mostly refused them. The timing must have been right, something for everyone to look forward to instead of the gloom that had overtaken all aspects of life at casa Watkins. I don't know if Mrs. Watkins would have let her go out with an eleventh-grader under normal circumstances, but circumstances would never again be normal at Jamie's house. Mr. Watkins would never have let her go out.

Amber did go out with Robert Bonham, and he brought her home pretty close to when she was supposed to be back, and he was nice to Jamie, even okay to me, so they settled into the boyfriend-girlfriend thing rather than simply hooking up the way most kids did.

I'd known Amber for so long, but when I saw all the different clothes she tried on or how excited she was it sort of made me not want to be around her. It was like a different person. She'd turned into a chick, giggly and stupid and moody, depending upon what was up with Robert.

After they had been together for about six months, Amber baked him a cake for his birthday. The problem was she had just finished putting the icing on it when Jamie and I returned from surfing. We rode bikes that day, had surfed close, at Playa Chica, had surfed about five hours, and had ridden to and from the beach. We were hungry!

I saw Amber in her cutoff Levi's and pigeon-toed bare feet rush out of the kitchen as we entered. She was on her cell, I thought, and didn't want us to hear her conversation.

"Thank you, dear Lord," Jamie said, grabbing some plates and forks and a big knife from a drawer.

I was comfortable around Jamie's house but not enough to cut open a freshly baked cake. I could get glasses and milk, though, which I did. And I could eat it. I put the half gallon of milk right on the table with us.

"Oh, yeah," Jamie said. "This is fresh." Jamie's voice was usually low, though it could be high when he laughed. But when he was happy or excited his voice got higher, elevating everyone's mood.

He cut two huge pieces and we finished them in a second, washing them down with milk. As I watched him cut two more, I thought of what my father called Jamie: the skinny hog. Jamie could eat anything in sight but wouldn't gain weight. We finished the next two pieces as well, savoring the cake's warm, rich white texture contrasted with the chocolate icing.

"I'm hungry!" Jamie said. While smiling he cut what was left of the cake in half, placing one piece on my plate, the other on his. The skinny hog and his loyal sidekick.

I poured more milk. It wasn't up to me to monitor cake eating in the Watkins house.

We left the kitchen for his room after having finished the cake. We were just kicking it, relaxing and listening to music, when we heard Amber cussing. Soon Mrs. Watkins came charging into Jamie's room, blowing open the door like we'd killed the neighbor's dog or something.

"What's the matter with you two?" she shouted at us.

"Calm down," Jamie said, smirking.

Why is that with some people the madder they get, the funnier it becomes? Maybe because it's so out of place. Claire Watkins wasn't going to harm us. She was probably having trouble yelling at us. And that's what made it funny. That, and Amber's banging around the kitchen.

"What's the tragedy?" Jamie said in his high voice.

"You ate the cake Amber baked for Robert. The whole damn thing!" She was going to play tennis or something because she had on a tennis outfit but hadn't yet put up her hair or put on her shoes. She stood there in her ankle socks, her cheeks flushed and her blond hair swinging back and forth as she moved her head for emphasis.

"We didn't know it was for Robert," Jamie said, now struggling to withhold his laughter. Then he chuckled, and that opened the floodgates. His laugh was staccato and his shoulders jumped up and down slightly and his whole face scrunched up so that his eyes were slits.

I didn't know why the fact that Amber had made the cake for Robert made it funnier, but it did. And then when Amber showed up at the doorway glaring at us, we got an even bigger case of the giggles.

"You dork, Juan!" she shouted at me. "Asshole," she sneered at Jamie.

That made Jamie roll off his bed onto the floor, overtaken with laughter.

"Watch your language, Amber," Mrs. Watkins said. "It's not funny, Jamie, Juan," she said, trying to add some dignity to the scene.

But we couldn't stop laughing, which was just getting us in deeper shit. Until Amber came in with a glass of water and threw it in Jamie's face, which didn't stop the laughter but got him off the floor as he chased her out of the room. Down the hall, I heard Amber shouting, "You're both assholes! Assholes!"

When I stood up I was pretty close to Mrs. Watkins. I could smell her coconut body lotion and could see that her blouse wasn't yet buttoned all the way, could just see some freckles on her chest by her throat. I was taller than she was, only recently having overtaken her. Jamie was almost a head taller than his mother.

She had looked in my eyes, and hers had clouded up, and I thought she was going to cry. But she didn't; a smile broke out instead, and she mouthed the word *thanks* without uttering a sound, and turned on her heel and walked out. I didn't know what she meant but I was glad that she didn't cry, because I wouldn't have known what to do.

I chuckled thinking of that cake and that time. But I also wondered if Mrs. Watkins would thank me now. I knew the answer to that question.

Riding up to his house, I saw the freestanding basketball hoop Mr. Watkins had bought a thousand years ago lying on its side, blocking the driveway, probably knocked over by neighborhood kids. All the roses were dead and withered, the flower beds filled with weeds, the hedges overgrown and unkempt, the lawn dead with patches of dirt and mud everywhere.

I rode right up to the front door, where I rang the doorbell. It didn't work so I knocked. First softly with my knuckles, then using the side of my fist. I banged harder and harder, willing a Watkins to appear. I kept banging until my right fist hurt; then I used my left one.

"They don't live there anymore!" the across-the-street neighbor shouted. An older guy watering his flowers. "Nobody lives there."

I saw that guy over a period of years, saw him go from what I thought was an old guy to a very old guy. He didn't know me from shit, it seemed. "Okay," I whispered. I knew everything was over.

Riding back over the dead lawn past the downed backboard, I knew Jamie was gone.

∽

As the days became longer, I became resigned to the fact that he was gone. It was gradual, first a vague sensation, then a creeping realization. I knew Amber was not around geographically, and though that hurt, I could accept it. But Jamie. I was responsible for him. I wasn't a hero, though in the heat of the moment I thought my actions were appropriate. It turned out they weren't, and they culminated in the drowning of my friend. And Amber. How had my actions affected her? If we hadn't run? If I hadn't stolen my mother's car?

∽

My lawyer told my parents that F was getting better with therapy. Sort of. I mean, he wasn't a slobbering vegetable or anything. He did use a walker; I had seen that much, though I'd heard that he no longer had to use it.

At some point the police had talked with him about the fight with Jamie. Or the D.A. had, my lawyer said. Everything weird that happened was good for me, my lawyer said. All the complexities of the case, and of the Watkins family, were good for me, my lawyer said.

I think F cruised by my house once, but I'm not sure. It was when I was getting the mail from the box out on the road that I saw a car off in the distance. It was going real slow, idling forward, it seemed. And then it stopped. I looked at the car, but there was a glare off the windshield and I couldn't see who was driving. It was a car like F's, I think, and it gave me the creeps.

I wonder if that means Claire Watkins won't ever take him back? She was in Oklahoma to be with Amber; she'd told my mother she was leaving California, and F.

The D.A. hadn't committed to anything one way or the other regarding Jamie and F's fight. And the Mexican Consulate finally produced an official letter stating that they couldn't find anything out of the way about Jamie. In the letter there was some speculation about a drowning, no speculation about foul play, but nothing conclusive. All these things were great for me, my lawyer said, and subsequently he was able to negotiate a plea bargain, which placed me on two years' probation. If I didn't do anything to break my probation, the judgment would be expunged from my record when I was eighteen.

And that was that. Sort of. Yet there was no final resolution, no official statement or anything about Jamie. There was no funeral service or memorial service, nothing. He simply disappeared into bureaucratic indifference. He no longer existed because of government agencies that were too low on funds to pursue the matter.

I could get on with my life, the court commissioner assigned to my case told me. Since Nestor still had me grounded and since I couldn't surf even if I wanted to, which I didn't, my life could not go on. I would have to go back to school now, unless I wanted to remain in independent study forever, which I didn't.

The psychiatrist the court ordered me to see as part of my probation told me to make up different scenarios about what happened. Unlike Ms. Catrone, I could talk with this guy. One scenario I made up was a dual family vacation, in which Amber and I got to do all the stuff we did, and Jamie got to do everything he did, but we all came home and resumed our lives in a fashion similar to how we once lived. We returned, and Amber was my girlfriend. Jamie was the big stud surfer who'd ridden the biggest wave ever.

In another scenario my father accompanied me back to La Isla de los Delfins. He believed me about the island. And when we returned, the dolphins were still there, and Jamie's board was on the beach, and I surfed in that bay while my father watched, and I swore that Jamie's presence was there, swore that I could see him in the waves with me, tucked back inside the tube, dolphin-kicking.

I also tried to remember accurately what happened, another suggestion from the psychiatrist. But it was hard to be truthful.

Here were the facts: the image of Jamie freefalling down that horrendous wave will be in my psyche forever. I didn't remember much of that day after the outside reef broke. Amber pulled me from the surf, barely conscious, vomiting and shivering. She claimed a dolphin had swum me in to shallow water. I remembered nothing of that. When I came around, no matter how hard or where we searched, we found nothing of Jamie or his board. Jamie was drowned; Amber was married; I was on probation.

The psychiatrist also told my parents that it wasn't right that I hadn't cried. At first I thought I might tear up over any little thing, and then when I refused to believe that Jamie was gone, it was easy not to cry. Even when I found out that Robert Bonham and Amber were married, I didn't cry.

I was supposed to prepare myself mentally to return to school, though all I did was ruminate about the trip, and the surfboards were a tangible link to that time and place, I supposed. And to make my life go on, it seemed, I cared for the boards. Maybe that was the starting point. Mine sat in the garage, gleaming its resin shine, though its nose was broken, a perpetual reminder of my notorious surf trip. Placing Amber's board in the sun and leaning it against a trash can with the middle fin on a cushion, I prepared to work on it. The sun was hot and almost immediately it began to melt the wax. My mother had given me one of her old spatulas, which worked well for removing the wax off a surfboard.

Straddling Amber's board, I took the spatula and with the edge worked down from the nose to the tail. A big gob of wax formed on the spatula. I flicked it off into the dirt by the trash cans. After two passes straddling the board, I could work on one side, which I did, removing the wax. There were a bunch of shatters on her board's blue edges, I noticed, as the disappearing wax revealed what was truly underneath. Her stringer was fine, though; no water taken in. Another time I will seal the shatters, along with all the ones on my board. The shatters were from hitting the beach. The boards were all I had left, and it seemed as if the events from the recent past were truly only a dream. After I seal the shatters I'll polish both boards. Something to do since I didn't surf anymore.

I cleaned the spatula with a cloth. Then went over the entire surface of the board, removing any wax spots that I hadn't gotten. As I worked over the board sweat dripped onto the deck. The hot May sun burned my back and neck, but I didn't care. I just went over and over the deck's surface, as if removing every speck of wax could somehow right things. After a number of passes with the spatula, I wiped down the entire surface of the board, top and bottom. Then I got out the acetone and continued to rub the fiberglass surface. The sweet smell of the acetone coupled with the afternoon heat and the fact that I hadn't eaten all day made me woozy. But, still, I kept my arms moving.

Oftentimes I was aware of Amber's presence. I felt her holding me in the warm sand with the water's explosions going off all around us. And sometimes I awakened in the night, thinking that she and I were lying together, but we weren't. Sometimes when I closed my eyes I saw Jamie taking that endless drop, weightless; saw him falling, falling down the face of that humongous wave, his feet firmly planted on the deck of his board, even though his board was not *in* water as that massive barrel overtook him. I saw him take the drop. I saw the white universe approaching me. When I relaxed and didn't focus and let the images flow through my mind, sometimes I felt the presence of dolphins, as Amber said. But it was nothing definite.

I took Amber's board into the garage, placing it on top of mine and covering it with an old blanket. Then I went over to the block wall and climbed on top of it, looking at the ocean. The swell was building, and I saw the steady lines of whitewater at the beach. The first south swell of the season, the first of the water from the southern hemisphere.

Much of the time I was scared, and especially now, as I would be going back to school tomorrow. I didn't know how the other kids would treat me. I wouldn't have my best friend with me, and Amber wouldn't be around. I did know this: nothing would ever be the same again. I was responsible for Jamie's drowning. If I hadn't taken my mother's car . . .

But I had already been taught the greatest lesson of them all: loss. The loss of my best friend; the loss of the girl I loved.

The psychiatrist said that I must accept Jamie's death, and that I must accept the fact that Amber was gone; I had.

As I turned to leave the wall after having looked at the waves, Nestor and my mother were suddenly there. Bonnie had gone into labor, and my parents had been at the hospital with Raul. "You're an uncle," my mother said.

I smiled. "What's his name?" We'd known the sex of the baby.

"James," Nestor said. Bonnie's father's name.

I looked up into the blue afternoon sky, seeing a few streamer clouds scudding along, hearing seagulls squawking down at the beach, smelling the salt air chugging in over the mesa, and I didn't know what gave because suddenly Nestor was holding me, squeezing me tightly, and my whole body was shaking and my face was wet and I couldn't stop sobbing, just like some damn baby.

"There, mi'jo," he said, and I felt his strong embrace cover me like a tube.

CHAPTER 18

I'm bored already at school, as usual, even though I haven't been here, like, since forever. Mr. Vance, my tenth-grade English teacher, is droning on about Dickens and Pip. He embarrassed me earlier when he welcomed me back. He was all worked up, his face red, and spittle flying all over the front of the room. He was saying stuff like, "You guys have to face your challenges. There are no obstacles, only possibilities. Everybody makes mistakes. It's what we do with our knowledge of those mistakes that counts." Crap like that, which made everyone in my class squirm, not just me. And using me as an example! Saying that I surfed and I was going to college (we'll see about that, if I can salvage this year) and I was Latino to boot! That's what I get for always getting A's in English. What I get for being in the H classes.

Now, thank God, he's simply boring.

Susan Cohen rolls her eyes at me and Sylvia Cisneros touches my arm as she walks by my desk when the bell rings. Mr. Vance calls to me, but I pretend not to hear him and keep walking. Home-room is over.

In the halls nobody seems too concerned that I'm back, though Greg J., the surf team god, goes out of his way to acknowledge me. Some of my school friends ask "what's up?" as they pass, like I haven't been gone forever. I sit alone in the back of my next class, history, while Ms. Scanlen goes on and on about some revolution. The room's door across the hall is open, and Herbie French sits there, bored stiff too. I flip him off every time Ms. Scanlen isn't looking. I have to focus my attention toward the front of the room, flipping off Herbie "blind." When Ms. Scanlen looks at the class, I can turn my gaze at Herbie, who in turn flips me off when his teacher, Mr. Evans, isn't looking. When I last flip off Herbie and look over at him, who's standing there but Mr. Evans, one of a few black teachers at our school. He shakes his head and closes the door on me. I flipped off Mr. Evans! And I can see Herbie with his head on the desk, stifling his laughter. Mr. Evans is cool; Ms. Scanlen is a boor.

And so the day progresses in a somewhat usual way. Except that Jamie isn't here.

When school's over I walk down to the pier. Greg Scott and Herbie and some other guys I know are in the water. I haven't been out in so long and it feels weird to watch my friends surf from up on the pier, a thing that only tourists do.

I thought a lot about surfing when I was stuck at home, and I wonder if Amber surfs anymore. I don't think there are waves in Oklahoma, but you never know these days. When I thought about when I would get back in the water I'd wonder, Why will I get a second chance, a second surfing life? Jamie doesn't surf. Or maybe he's perpetually surfing. Maybe time stops when you die; maybe it's like the moment when entering wavetime and everything's frozen, maybe that's what death is and Jamie is forever in that place on that wave. That would be heaven for Jamie, to be in the prime moment, the second that everything and nothing are the same. That's where Jamie is: taking the drop on a wave on an island.

As I daydream, watching the water move through the pier, I hear Greg Scott yell, "Come on out, Juan!"

The waves are decent, about four feet on the sets, looking fun. And there is some power to them, the swell generated far down in the southern hemisphere, traveling across the seas, hitting our shore.

"No board!" I shout down to him.

"You can use mine. C'mon, get in the water."

"Can't. I'm not supposed to."

"Shit," Herbie yells, as if what we're supposed to do and what we actually do have any connection. He takes off on a cool little three-foot line, working it all the way until it peters out next to the pilings.

Greg Scott rides in, waving me down to the beach, once he's on it.

"I don't even have a wetsuit, dude," I say.

"Look." He points down to the pile of stuff, backpacks and towels and who knows what, and there's a wetsuit. "Ricky was here but he split. He won't care."

And so with Ricky Ybarra's wetsuit and Greg Scott's board, I paddle out, even though I'm still technically grounded. But Nestor is softening toward me, I know by what happened yesterday. I paddle close to the pier, and I can hear the waves' soft echo as they stream through the pilings. I can hear guys paddling, the slap of their hands on the ocean's surface as they take off, can hear the rush of water as the waves fold over themselves, and I can feel the warm sun on my back and the refreshing cool of the sea as it passes over me on the paddle out. Off in the distance I can see pelicans and gulls fishing. Three dolphins break the surface out beyond the surf line, heading south, blowing air out their blowholes as they arch back down into the water.

As I get into the lineup, and with the image of the dolphins still in my mind's eye, I take off on the first wave of a set. My friends let me have it — in fact they seem happy that I am out. I stroke for all I'm worth, heading toward shore as the wave tries to beat me, but it doesn't, I catch it, and as it starts to feather over, I stand up, and I'm weightless. . . .

ACKNOWLEDGMENTS

Special thanks to Alvina Ling for her patience, kindness,
and gracious suggestions for editing this book.
Thanks to Ricardo Means Ybarra and Sean Carswell for
their insightful reads of the manuscripts, their knowledge
of surfing, and their friendship.
And, as always, thanks to Pat, my first reader.